Veiled Intentions

Kate Allenton

Discover other titles by Kate Allenton

At

www.kateallenton.com

DEDICATION

This book is dedicated to all of the readers that still believe in true love.

May you have the courage to follow your heart, just like Sophie.

1 CHAPTER

Sophie stepped up to the receptionist at the police department and mustered a sweet smile. There was nothing unusual about her visits. Her brother was chief after all. Today was different. This wasn't a friendly visit, not when she was catching the bastards red-handed.

"Where are they?" she asked.

Veronica grinned and gestured with a nod toward the conference room door. "Boy, what I wouldn't give to be a fly on the wall."

Sophie pressed her lips together and headed toward where the traitors were meeting. She swung the door open and placed her hand on her hip. "What did I miss?"

The exchanged glances would have been comical if the reason they were meeting wasn't so important. The Pentagram killer was back and had struck again…and this time it was in *her* town.

Marshall rose. "Sophie, what are you doing here? I thought you were having lunch with Amber."

"Our lunch meeting got pushed back." She let her gaze sweep the room, noting her brother, Jack, and Cord were also in attendance. "It's a good thing too. I might have missed this."

Jack stood up. "Uh-uh, no way in hell is she helping on this one."

"Sit down, Love," her brother, Max, ordered before he returned his gaze to Marshall, her boyfriend slash boss. She'd expected Jack's refusal, and maybe a little flak from her brother if she was being honest, but the fact that they'd tried to blackball her out of this case had every nerve ending on fire. If she had superpowers, she'd be shooting cobwebs out of her hands to cover their mouths to keep them from lying to her face. "She's not doing this."

An apparition appeared in the room, standing at the other end of the table. The boisterous woman who Sophie had met while learning about her clairvoyance, wore the standard-issue white coven dress. A dress that Sophie knew all too well. The apparition wasn't just a member of the spiritual coven. She had been their leader.

"He struck again?" she asked, returning her gaze to Marshall.

Silence greeted her. Interesting.

She turned her questioning to her brother. "Mary James," she stated more than asked. "Head of the local coven."

Jack's eyes narrowed. "How do you know that? It isn't public information."

Marshall retook his seat and leaned backward in his chair, a half grin on his face, a glimmer of pride showed in his eyes. "Do you even have to ask, Jack?"

Sophie blew Marshall a kiss before gesturing toward the end of the table. "She's standing right there." Sophie put her hand on the doorknob and grinned. Her work here was done. Validation and vindication acquired. "I guess since I wasn't invited to your little party I'll go have my own."

Turning, she wiggled her fingers. "Tootles."

Sophie left the men to contemplate her visit. Her fight was far from over because she was just getting started. Sophie slid into the back seat of the waiting Dixon Security SUV. Beau was behind the wheel; Amber riding shotgun, and Aiden was behind her.

Aiden grinned. "How did it go?"

"You know..." was her only reply. She shrugged her shoulders.

Amber turned around in her seat. "That good?"

"You have to give Cord a break because he's new, but the others.... They should have known better than to try keeping this case from you," Beau announced.

Aiden laid his arm across the back of the seat. "Oh, I don't know. I can see why they're worried

3

about her. Their only mistake is underestimating my mad teaching skills."

"Conceited much?" Beau asked while adjusting the rearview mirror to see Aiden's face.

"She can take your ass." Aiden smirked.

"Any time, any place," Beau replied.

Amber tapped Beau on the arm. "You are not allowed to hurt my best friend."

"But, baby…he's practically daring me."

"I'm not afraid of him, Amber." Sophie winked at Aiden. "Aiden is that good."

"That's my girl." He rubbed her shoulder. "So where are we going for lunch."

"Mexican," they all replied at the same time.

****

Twenty minutes later they were seated at their local favorite restaurant and each had the best nachos in town sitting in front of them. The heavenly melted cheesy gooeyness was too good to share.

"You know what I don't get," Sophie said. "How they thought they could keep me out of it."

Beau shrugged. "The Pentagram Killer is dangerous and elusive. I'm sure they were just worried."

Sophie took a sip of her sweet iced tea. "You guys aren't."

"Think about who was in the meeting, Soph. Your ex-boyfriend, your new boyfriend, your brother and your new trainee who, by the way, deserves a good reprimand for not warning you. You are a partner after all. Marshall should have brought it to the table. We should have agreed as a unit."

"We may be partners, but he still owns the majority vote," she countered.

"He's also thinking with his johnson instead of his head."

"And that's unusual?" Amber cheerfully asked.

Aiden chuckled as he glanced at Sophie. "If you were my girlfriend, I wouldn't want you anywhere near the case either."

"Good thing I'm not." She smirked and leaned back in the booth, her food momentarily forgotten. "This was exactly what I was afraid would happen."

Amber swallowed the nacho in her mouth. "You can always break up with him. It's not like he's giving you any."

Aiden and Beau paused with chips halfway to their mouths. They turned to stare at her with wide eyes.

"You had to go there," Sophie relied incredulously. Her best friend was right, but it was Sophie's sex life after all. She didn't need her partners knowing.

"What? It's the truth. He brings a whole new meaning to the phrase 'putting a ring on it.'"

"Is that why you've been so cranky?" Beau's lips twitched. "You need to get laid?"

Aiden slid his arm around her shoulders and squeezed her into his side. "Do you need me to take the edge off? It can be our little secret."

"I suggest your remove your hand if you want to keep it, Aiden." Marshall strolled up to the table. He pulled a chair over to their booth and twisted it around to sit backward. Marshall was a good-looking man. He looked great every day, but there was something special about him today. Was it that she was seeing him through rose-colored glasses?

Aiden removed his hand but kept his shit-eating grin. "Just thought you might need some help with your girl." Aiden shot a mischievous look toward Beau before returning his gaze to Marshall. "We hear you aren't performing."

"Oh, for the love of god…" Sophie cupped her reddened face in her hands. "I did not say that."

Marshall took one of Sophie's nachos and shoved the entire thing into his mouth. He chewed and swallowed before standing. Leaning over her, he pressed his hot mouth to hers in a kiss that could make her forget they were in public. Her insides turned to mush. He tasted of cheese and gooeyness and everything she loved. His kiss made her body ache. A moan slipped from her lips. His fingers glided over her neck before tangling in her hair. There was no hesitation, only a deepening demand. His tongue slid into her mouth, possessing and making her question her hesitation on giving into the one thing he wanted. A simple yes and he'd take her. A simple yes and he'd fill her. A simple yes and her life wouldn't be her own.

She pressed at his chest. He grinned against her lips. He didn't budge, but he ended the kiss with a few nibbles on her lower lip. Her cheeks flushed and her lips tingled. "I'm mad at you."

"I know." He leaned his forehead against hers and whispered, "I'm sorry."

Sophie chewed her lip for a split second, hoping that her hesitation would stop him from making the same mistake again. He needed proper training in everything a boss and boyfriend should and shouldn't do. Oh, who was she kidding? At his first grin in the conference room, she'd forgiven him. She smiled, letting him off the hook. "Apology accepted. Don't be an idiot again."

Marshall pressed a tiny kiss to her lips before righting his stance. He used a finger to draw a cross over his heart. "Cross my heart. Scout's honor."

"I seriously doubt you were a scout," she teased.

The twinkle in his eyes hinted that she was right. He was one big mystery she was determined to solve and knew that she'd love every minute of it. "When you get back to the office, I'll fill you in on the file."

Marshall strolled toward the door and called over his shoulder, "Keep your paws off my girl."

"That's her call," Aiden hollered back.

"Dude…" Sophie picked up another nacho and pulled at the cheese on top. "Don't poke the bear. He's just as sexually frustrated as I am, if not more." She grinned.

****

Sophie arrived back at work and dropped her purse off behind her desk before heading to Marshall's office. She took the long route and strolled by Cord's desk, holding his gaze as she passed. Unafraid of his six-foot-two frame and the lethal scowl permanently etched on his face, she gestured, pointing from her eyes back to his in quick succession. "You and me....later."

Marshall's door was open. He stood lost in thought behind his desk, looking out of the tinted floor-to-ceiling window to the street below. Butterflies took flight in her belly every time she was near him. She admired his gorgeous body, but also his beautiful mind and heart too. His large hands were clasped behind his back, his dark Armani suit tailored to fit every inch of his body. The material was expensive and beautiful, but it didn't compare to the man wearing it.

"Like the view?" he asked.

"Better than yours." She walked up to stand next to him. She lowered her gaze to the street below to figure out what was holding his attention.

"He could be anyone," Marshall announced out of the blue. "We don't even have a face to look at, much less a name."

"He could be a she," Sophie countered.

"Doubt it." Marshall moved to stand behind her and wrapped his arms around her waist. He rested his head on her shoulder before placing a tiny kiss on her neck. "She'd have to be a body builder, due to the sheer size of some of the guys killed in the past, not to mention the positions they were left in."

Sophie placed her arms on top of Marshall's and stroked circles, enjoying the feel of the material. A white dove landed on the windowsill outside. "We may be looking at a team, possibly a couple."

Marshall raised his head, glancing down at the side of her face. "Why do you say that?"

She shrugged and turned to steal a kiss. "Only another harmless-looking female could have gotten close enough to lure Mary away from her coven. She was a smart and wise woman, so we're dealing with someone unassuming."

She turned in his arms and laced her fingers behind his neck. "You need me."

"I've known that since the first day I met you."

She rose up on her tiptoes and pressed another kiss to his lips. "That's not what I meant. You need me on this case."

She cupped his cheeks and stole another kiss before she sidestepped him and headed for the door. "Family meeting in thirty minutes. We vote." She turned at the last minute and grinned. "I already have three votes in my pocket, so get ready to concede."

"Sophie. Do what you will, but you're the one that may be eating crow." Marshall's eyes glinted with secrets, his smile assuring her that he meant what he said.

"Marshall, honey….there isn't much that can surprise me."

"We'll see." He winked before turning back toward the window and reassuming the position he'd been in before she interrupted.

2 CHAPTER

Sophie was the first one in the meeting room, already in her seat. Her mind replaying the first time she'd walked into the room and how far she'd come since then. Four men, four of the most gorgeous men she'd ever met, had stared at her on the first day of her new job. They'd joked; they'd teased; they'd flirted; and now...they were her equals. She'd saved two lives and earned their respect and trust. Today she was putting that loyalty to the test to see if they'd meant what they said, or if their words were nothing more than empty promises.

They all started piling in, joking and bantering like a bunch of kids coming off the playground. They each took a seat; Marshall was two minutes behind them. He had a large box he set on the floor near his chair. He stood at the end of the table. Sophie started to say something, but he held up his hand.

"I need to explain something first, before you have your vote."

Sophie eased back into her chair, not liking that Marshall had the floor. His words were powerful and decisive. Him talking first might sway some of the group, but Aiden and Beau promised they were on her side. She sat there and let him continue. What other choice did she have?

"Some of you may have noticed that I had a meeting with the police this morning."

Sophie narrowed her eyes and crossed her arms over her chest, not liking the way the meeting was starting. He'd dived right in, striking at the heart of the matter. She was impressed, even though a tinge of worry crept up her spine. Whatever his game was, he wouldn't win.

"Well, they've asked for our help on some cold cases."

Sophie slowly shook her head, her lips pressed hard in a sour-puss smirk to keep from running off at the mouth. If he thought for one minute he was going to stick her in that ungodly little room with another officer like Jack or, worse, Jack himself, then Marshall had another thing coming. Game on.

Marshall smiled at her and quirked his brows playfully while holding her gaze. "You don't even know what I'm going to say and you're shaking your head no."

She watched him with smug delight and waved her hand. "Don't let me stop you; please continue."

They exchanged a subtle look of amusement before he continued. "As I was saying, they need our help on a few things. One, being the cold cases and the other, the recent killing."

"The cold cases are understandable, but why the killing?" Roman, the notoriously quiet team leader, asked from his spot at the other end of the table.

Marshall held up his hand, staying the question. "I'm getting to that. Let's discuss the cold cases first. I'd like to send Cord in to help." Marshall directed his gaze toward Sophie. "He's in your department. Do you object to me sending him into the field to test out his clairvoyant abilities?"

Sophie's mouth parted. Confusion clouded her mind, and then the bastard winked, rubbing in that he'd gained the upper hand. Touché, boss man. "As long as he reports in with his findings, I don't object. I think it will help him progress."

Marshall shifted his gaze around the room to the rest of the guys. "Anyone object?"

They all shook their heads. Marshall clapped his hands.

"Great. Now, second order of business." He lifted the box to sit it on the table in front of him. His fingers tapped the lid, yet he left it closed. "The other killing in question is the coven leader. The style of the kill indicates that it was the Pentagram Killer."

"How do you know you aren't dealing with a copycat, like the cold case Sophie already solved?" Dash asked.

Marshall opened the box and pulled out several pictures from the top. He tossed them on the table. She and each of the guys picked one up. Every picture was different; the one she had was of Mary, the local leader. The dead local leader.

"The police and I assumed that there wasn't a pattern." He shrugged. "Well, there wasn't one we could see, until recently. Each person killed was missing a significant piece of jewelry. From the men, it was rings with the initials of the covens they belonged to and, for the women, it was a pendant."

Sophie's mouth dropped open. "The Celtic knot?"

An easy smile played at the corners of Marshall's mouth. "How did you know that?"

"Mary showed me hers. It has her name on the back. It's given to the leaders and prominent members of the coven."

Marshall continued by pointing to the remaining pictures sitting in the middle of the table. "Each was a practicing witch or had psychic abilities; each of them, although varying in many aspects, including occupations, had one major common thread that, until recently, went unnoticed."

Sophie leaned back in her chair and tilted her head to the side, unsure where Marshall was headed. Marshall's grin grew bigger by the second.

"And?" Aiden asked.

"And…they were all members of a similar coven, much like our local one," Marshall continued.

"That explains the jewelry," Sophie added. The implications swirled through her mind. Who was next? Her gaze strayed back to the picture of Mary.

Her neck was bare except for a tiny puncture wound.

Beau leaned forward in his chair with renewed interest. "We're going in under cover?"

Marshall took two dresses out of the box. One white and the other black. The material was one she recognized immediately. He walked around to stand behind her and laid them on the table in front of her. "Piper Gray, the interim coven leader, has already contacted us to ask for help with the police investigation into Mary's death, so we've already put the ball in motion. Sophie is going in undercover."

Sophie's eyes widened and her throat turned dry. Marshall had managed to render her speechless. There was a first time for everything. He was good, very good. She'd underestimated Marshall Dixon's abilities. The man was just full of surprises.

Finding her voice, she glanced up at him. "Seriously?"

He nodded. "Only you might change your mind after you hear the other common thread we've noticed."

Her momentary hope started to fade. "What's the other?"

"The other was they were married. And not only that, but their spouses didn't have any ability."

"I'm not marrying you," she stubbornly announced. If this was some ploy to get his way, he was mistaken.

He chuckled. "Not yet, anyway."

15

Marshall finally sat down and moved the box back to the floor. "Sophie and I are going undercover as husband and wife. It's already been arranged. We'll have all of the appropriate paperwork..." He glanced at her, the twinkle snuffed out and sadness reflected in his eyes. "Even if it isn't real."

"What makes you think we can just walk in there? They aren't going to trust us." Sophie had first-hand knowledge of how hard it had been to get information from the group to solve her very first cold case.

"That's where you're wrong, darling. Piper requested our help. It seems they need a clairvoyant or a psychic, and we just happen to have one. The woman believes it was an inside job."

Sophie collapsed back in her chair.

He glanced around the room. "Let's vote."

Marshall held up his hand and peered at the others. "I vote we take the case and Sophie and I go under cover."

The rest of the guys looked at her expectantly. "Sophie, what do you want to do?" Dash asked.

"It's your decision. This is your life; your safety going on the line. We'll back you 100 percent on whatever your decision is," Aiden added.

Roman and Beau nodded their agreement.

Sophie didn't have to think long or hard about it. The Pentagram Killer had already tried to kill Jack and was going after innocent people with the same ability that she also had.

"I vote yes." She raised her hand to match Marshall's.

They all responded the same.

That day, she had a newfound appreciation for Marshall Dixon. He not only believed in her, he wanted to help her. She'd jumped to conclusions at the police station, unfounded conclusions. Every day she noticed something new about him, whether it was something he did or said. A kiss here, a word of encouragement there, he was always keeping her off guard. She was beginning to not only believe he wanted to marry her, but that he might possibly love her, although he'd never said the words.

And here she was agreeing to play the part of his wife. What the hell had she just agreed to? A shiver of apprehension skirted her spine. Could she play the part and keep her heart intact? Or would she succumb to him once and for all, losing her independence in the process? This idea sucked balls. Either way she lost.

Marshall adjourned the meeting and she waited for the rest of the partners to walk out. She sat in her chair, her gaze holding Marshall's until they were by themselves.

He shut the conference room door and retook his seat.

"We need boundaries," she announced.

His green eyes glinted with quick humor. "What kind of boundaries? We don't have them now, unless it's the one I imposed."

"No sex until I agreed to marry you." She rose from her chair and grinned. He thought he had her, that he was the only one holding the cards. She walked over to where he sat, placed her palms on

17

each of the chair arms, and leaned down so she could look him in the eyes when she spoke.

"I believe you're the one who just pointed out that I'm about to be your wife." She winked. "Even if it isn't real, I'll have the paperwork to prove it." She pressed her lips to his. "I'll be over at eight." Checkmate.

"Sophie, you know I meant the real deal."

"Sorry, *darling,* you didn't specify the logistics when you made the deal. As I recall, you said not until I agreed to marry you." She pressed an even slower kiss to his lips, savoring his taste mixing with hers. "I just did, in front of witnesses, so now it's time to hold up your end of the deal."

He rose, crowding her as he stood. His palms found her waist and he pulled her to his chest. "Honey, don't start something you can't finish."

She cupped him through his suit, stroking him nice and slow. "Oh, I plan on finishing…and I plan to take you over the edge with me." She stopped stroking and stepped back. "Enjoy the rest of your day. I'll see you tonight."

She left him standing in the conference room. Her panties were wet with anticipation. She glanced at her watch. She had six long, grueling hours to wait before she planned to meet him. Six long, grueling hours of hoping she could stop herself from storming into his office, offering up her body as a snack, and letting him take her on the top of his mahogany desk.

Bad Sophie, she scolded as images skirted in her mind. She grinned. "Bad, bad Sophie, indeed."

The day dragged on, making it appear as though time had slowed down. She'd had her well-meaning talk with Cord, explaining that, even though Marshall was the big boss, she was next in line and anything requested of him regarding special assignments was to be run through her. She was responsible for him; she was the one who was supposed to be grooming him, as if that were possible. He could kick her ass in mere seconds, yet the mention of talking to the dead had piqued his curiosity.

Sophie watched the last three minutes before the clock hit five. Time lingered and her anticipation threatened to boil over. The clock finally struck quitting time, and she grabbed her purse and made a beeline for the elevator to head down into the parking garage. The doors slid open and she stepped out. Marshall had his SUV parked right in front of the elevator, the passenger door wide open.

"Get in," he growled through gritted teeth.

"It's not eight and I have to run errands," she replied teasingly. Desire flashed in his eyes, as deep as the anticipation clawing at her skin.

"Sophie, get in or I'll take you right here, right now."

She batted her lashes and smiled. Marshall's door swung open and he was about to step out and come around toward her side. She slid into the passenger seat before he could make good on his promise. She closed the door and grinned while buckling her seat belt. She was in for a bumpy, fast ride, in more ways than one. "What happened to all that resolve you have?"

He pulled his door closed and paused, taking a deep breath before he shoved the SUV into gear. "I plan on showing you just how strong that resolve is. I hope you're ready." He glanced at her and a smile split his lips. "Be careful what you ask for, *darling*."

He pulled out of the parking garage and drove toward his house. His hand was on her knee, slowly moving up her thigh and beneath her skirt. The idea of his eagerness excited her, intensifying her need.

"Are you wet?" he asked.

"I'll never tell," she answered.

Marshall's fingers teased the elastic of her panties before he slid them to the side, sliding his finger through her drenched folds. She bit her lip, denying him the sound of her moans. His hungry gaze turned to her. "You are."

Marshall turned down his drive and killed the ignition. He was out of the SUV before she could unbuckle her seat belt. He opened her door and held out his hand in invitation. She took her time, teasing him even more. She wanted this. He wanted this. Fireworks were about to explode.

She stepped out of the SUV. His fingers pressed against her back, guiding her up the steps.

"Last chance to back out, Sophie." He slid his key into the lock and escorted her in. He disarmed his alarm and locked the door behind them.

He pressed her to the door, his hands on her waist, caressing up her body until he reached her face. His palms cupped her and his face softened. "Tell me to stop and I'll wait until you're ready."

His eyes searched hers as if trying to see to her soul. All of the frantic need and tension eased from his shoulders, and she wanted him more in that one minute, from that one statement, than she'd ever wanted another man. She wanted him to take her to bed.

"I can't think of anything I want more than you, Marshall. I want to feel you inside of me, making love to me."

She could tell the minute he'd come to his decision. He swooped her up into his arms and held her against his chest before heading toward his room.

"Why are you carrying me? Are you afraid I'm going to run away?"

He smiled and kicked the bedroom door shut. "I want to savor the first time."

"Um…I hate to break it to you, but I'm not a virgin. That boat sailed during my teen years."

He chuckled, easing her body to slide down his until her feet were on the floor. He never let go. She looked into his eyes. The same smoldering emotions she held were reflected back at her.

He pulled her against his chest and dipped his head, his breath mixing and mingling with hers. "Sophie…"

She closed the distance between them, pressing her lips to his. "The time for talk is over," she murmured against his lips. She continued the assault until he eased and took the lead, sipping, tasting, and taking everything she had. His tongue stroked hers boldly, devouring her. The hands at her waist gripped her tightly, and she could feel the unrestrained passion burning through him.

He eased the blouse free from her skirt, pulling it up so slowly she thought she'd go mad. His fingers unfastened the top button. His moves were deliberate and easy, toying with her as if he had all the time in the world. The gentleness of his touch, the heat of his fingers brushing against her skin, had a gush of moisture flooding her panties. Her pussy throbbed and ached, needing to stroked, to be filled. She needed him in ways he'd not yet given her.

She yanked the material out of his hands, too impatient to wait. Practically ripping the buttons off, she finished unfastening the garment and let it flutter to the floor. Sophie broke the kiss and stepped back, her lips throbbing and tingling from the fierceness of Marshall's possession. Kicking off her shoes, she was naked in five seconds flat.

"Impatient?" Marshall asked through his chuckle.

She stepped over to him and loosened the knot of this tie, easing it over his head. Sophie tossed it aside, not caring where it landed, as long as it wasn't on him anymore. The clothes needed to go. All of them. She couldn't wait to get her hands on his naked flesh; the muscles she liked to watch bunched and played as he moved. He was hers, all hers, and she was dying to have a taste.

Marshall's palms moved to her hips and slid up her sides before cupping her breasts. He dipped his head, taking one of her nipples into his mouth, the rasp of his five o'clock shadow gently abrading her soft skin. She moaned in pleasure. His hand gently squeezed her other breast, as if he were worried it would feel left out. Sophie reached for him and cupped the back of his head, her fingers sifting through his hair, holding him to her, afraid that he would stop. Liquid fire burned through her veins as need pulsed throughout her body.

Another moan slid free, but she continued her task of ridding him from the suit that only hours ago she'd appreciated. She pulled his shirt out of his pants and started working the buttons in a quicker pace than he'd been working hers. She pushed it off his shoulders and pried his hands away from her body long enough for the garment to puddle at his feet. Her fingers itched to feel his heated skin, and she stroked her palms up the broad expanse of his chest to rest on his shoulders, feeling the power in his body.

His fingers twisted in her hair, and he was about to pull her to him for another kiss, but she held firm. "Not until I get you undressed."

"Says who?"

She cupped him, sliding her hand over his bulge. "Says me."

He released his hold and dropped his hands to his sides, giving her the lead, a thing she was sure was hard for a man like him. The small gesture excited her more.

She hurried to get him undressed, unhooking his belt so she could pop the button. She lowered the zipper, her fingers softly stroking him as she went. Sophie bunched the fabric of his pants and his boxers in her grip and dropped to her knees, taking the fabric with her. His erection was long, hard, and thick, standing at attention in her face, and she couldn't help but lick her lips. She hungered for his taste, to feel the steely length of him sliding along her tongue. Her hold on the material dropped, and she reached for him, wrapping her slender fingers around his shaft. She licked her lips again, ready to take him into her mouth. He eased back.

"If you do that, I'll never last."

"What happened to that resolve?"

He kicked off his shoes, tossed his socks aside and stepped out of his pants. She didn't even have a moment to admire the beauty of him before he helped her up from the floor and walked her backward toward the bed. He laid her down, easing his body onto hers, his weight deliciously pressing her into the bed. She felt every hard ridge of him cushioned against her softer curves. He was powerful, strong, an alpha in every sense of the word, and she'd never been more turned on in her life.

"My resolve flew out the window the moment I felt how wet you were."

He crushed his lips to hers, his tongue demanding entrance, and she wrapped her legs around his waist, aching to feel him inside of her. Her nipples were pebbled, the friction from pressing and rubbing against his chest sending a zing straight to her clit. His cock pressed at her folds, and she spread her legs farther, wanting him to take her. Needing him to take her.

Marshall broke the kiss, his chest heaving.

"Give me a second." He reached into the bedside drawer and pulled out a condom. He tore it open with his teeth and leaned back to rest on his legs. He slid the barrier into place before resuming his position. The head of his cock nudged her opening, slightly parting her lips. She fought the urge to lift her hips, to take him inside of her by any means necessary. Instead, she waited. She felt the tension in his body and knew that he wanted her every bit as much as she wanted him. But would he take her? Or had he made it this far, only to change his mind?

"Longer next time," he promised before he plunged into her, seating himself to the hilt in one fluid motion, stealing the breath from her lungs.

Her body squeezed and tightened around him, molding to him like a glove. He filled her and claimed her, pressing against every nerve ending she had. Her inner walls clenched and unclenched, adjusting to his size, greedy for more.

His eyes hooded, his desire evident, he asked, "Are you okay?"

She nudged him with her ankles, wanting him, needing him to move.

He eased out of her slowly before pressing back in, the lines of his face intense as he took her. Moving his cock faster, in and out, he created the most amazing friction hitting all the right spots. Her toes curled in response. Her body heated, her desire for him blazing out of control.

Marshall reached between them, his thumb sliding over her clit in slow, tormenting circles, each stroke pushing her closer and closer to the edge, ratcheting up her need to match his.

"I need you to come with me." His voice was deep and husky, the warm tone like honey on her skin.

"Yes," she said breathlessly. Her channel clenched around him with the same intense need he was showing her, her desire, her need rising to a crest. Her body tightened in response, grasping for release.

"Marshall." She clutched his shoulders, digging her nails into his back. "I hope you're close."

Every muscle clenched as Marshall quickened the pace, slamming his cock into her with a fierce need that was more of a branding than anything else, the move leaving little doubt that she was his and only his. He sent her spiraling over the edge. Light fractured and time stopped. She screamed his name and he grunted hers. A few more quick strokes and he pressed into her, holding still. She felt the pulse of his shaft as he found the release he'd given her.

Several hours later, they made it out of bed long enough to eat before they continued their sexual explorations well into the night. Her muscles ached as she fell asleep, though only from pure exhaustion.

3 CHAPTER

Sophie showered and changed into some spare clothes she'd left at Marshall's house the last time she'd spent the night. Her gaze met Marshall's in the reflection of the mirror as she adjusted her earrings. He moved in behind her, leaning on the dresser, trapping her into place. He pressed a tender kiss on her neck. "Thank you."

She smiled. "Thank *you*."

He straightened and ran his palms up and down her arms, caressing her from behind. "I don't know what the hell I was thinking by making us wait."

"Aw,"—she turned to face him—"it was sweet." She kissed his lips. "Stupid, but sweet." She grinned.

"The office delivered the papers."

He pulled a diamond ring out of his pocket and held it up to her. Her breath caught. It was an antique, and it was amazing. A simple two-karat round diamond. The gold band was thick and accented with diamonds all the way around. If she ever picked out a ring for herself, this one would be hers.

"It's stunning." She looked up to find him watching her. She reached for it but paused with his next words.

"It was my grandmother's," he announced.

She pulled her hand back from the kryptonite, afraid a simple touch would burn. "I can't wear that."

"Why not?"

"Because it was your grandmother's."

"That's exactly why you're wearing it. It was my grandmother's and you're my wife."

"Fake wife."

He lifted her hand and slid the band onto her finger. "You needed a ring. I happen to have a ring." He grinned, leaning over to kiss her lips. His fingers rubbed where the ring sat on her hand. "Problem solved."

"What if I lose it?" she asked nervously.

"Then I'll replace it."

"Marshall." She slid it off her finger and set it down on the dresser. "I'm not wearing that ring."

"You're being difficult."

"Well, I *am* your wife." She grinned, throwing his words back at him.

"This is my first concession, Mrs. Dixon."

Her hand went to her chest. The name sounded foreign to her ears. "I'll forget to answer to that. Can't I be one of those independent women who keep their own name? And what are we going to do about our backstory?"

"We'll wing it." He grabbed a bag from the closet and started packing clothes inside. "As for the name, I guess we'll have to look at the paperwork. If you forget, just remind them that we're newlyweds. That should kill any suspicion. Pack for a week's stay and if we need more supplies then we'll make another trip into town."

She nodded and slid her hands into her pockets. "Great. All I need is my gun, some clothes, and a fake ring that, hopefully, won't turn my finger green."

"I think I can afford real gold, Sophie. But I won't even make it personal; we'll use one from the office." He grinned while packing his boxers. "I can't promise it'll be pretty."

"I didn't ask for pretty. I just need it to pass muster." Puzzled, she asked, "You keep rings at the office?"

"They're for kidnapping risks. They're traceable. I figure it couldn't hurt."

****

Two hours later, Sophie sat silently in the passenger seat of the SUV on the way to the coven compound located on the outskirts of town. She twisted the most horrific ring she'd ever seen on her finger. "Celebrities actually wore this gaudy thing? Why can't I get a plain band like yours?"

29

"Because a plain band wouldn't hide the tracker. Not only did the celebrities wear it, they showed it off. It's a designer ring and one of a kind."

"I bet Amber would love this."

He glanced at her like she was crazy.

"Well, she would."

Marshall slowed down at the entrance to the coven.

"Who knows the score?"

"Piper Gray. She stepped up as their leader to take control until the coven can vote on Mary's replacement."

"That makes it sound like a democracy."

Marshall parked the SUV and killed the ignition. "Are you ready for this?"

She nodded, though her belly was doing flips. She was walking into an even larger unknown than her ability to see spirits. What more was out there? Would it give her nightmares, or worse?

Marshall got out and rounded the SUV to open her door. He linked his hand into hers and headed toward the porch at the front of the main building on the compound.

Men and women stood in deep conversation, their voices barely above a whisper. Some just stood around drinking coffee in a zombie state, as if waiting for the caffeine to kick in. For a spiritual bunch, none were smiling; in fact, the looks they were getting weren't welcoming at all.

Marshall stopped just in front of the steps. "We're looking for Piper."

Conversations stopped, but no one answered him. The chilly reception did the opposite of making her want to flee. She bit her lip to keep from blurting they were rude. These people didn't know her or Marshall. The pricks.

Marshall slung his arm over Sophie's shoulders, pulling her into his side. "She's expecting us."

They all continued to look skeptically at them until an older woman stood and pushed through the center of the crowd. "Where are your manners?" she asked the others as she approached using her cane for support. . "I'm Vivian Baxter, but the folks around here just call me Nana."

Marshall shook her hand "I'm Marshall, and this is my wife, Sophie."

Nana stepped in front of Sophie and paused. "You look familiar." She waited to see if Sophie would reply. "Have you lived here before?"

Sophie shook her head. "Nope, I've visited Mary a time or two, but that's about it."

"Ah, that must be what it is. You two follow me, and I'll take you to Piper."

They followed behind the old woman into the building.

There were ten living people in the open room and yet another ten of the apparition variety. The door banged closed behind them, making Sophie's breath catch. The big open room was like a common area of sorts. With the ten people, there was enough room to move and breathe, but adding in all of the other presences, it was not only a bit overwhelming, but also draining. The energy in the room was electric and brimmed with life. Many turned to look at them, acknowledging their presence, and yet, some did not. Sophie pressed her lips together slowly taking in all of the occupants, memorizing each and who they were interacting with.

"Sophie?" Marshall asked.

"It's a little crowded?" Nana asked.

"You can see them too?" Sophie asked.

Nana nodded.

"I'm not sure I could handle this all day, every day."

Marshall glanced around, confused by the conversation, as if trying to figure it out.

Nana headed farther into the house down a long corridor. Old paintings lined the walls, but not much else, if you didn't count the wandering ghosts. Sophie wrapped her hand around Marshall's arm and whispered, "They're everywhere."

The old woman stopped outside of a closed door and turned the knob to push it open, not waiting for an invitation. "Piper, you have visitors."

Marshall and Sophie exchanged a glance. Did these people not believe in privacy? If so, it was possible one of them would get an eyeful if they decided to come find Sophie and Marshall after hours.

They stepped around Nana, thanking her as they entered the big office. Piper was Sophie's height, her brunette hair hung in waves reaching her shoulders. Beneath her pleasant smile and wise eyes, she permeated an air of authority. Piper lifted a leaf on the tall plant she was standing next to and squirted it with water. "Please come in and have a seat."

Nana left, pulling the door shut behind her. Marshall and Sophie moved around and sat in the chairs across from the desk.

Piper held her fingers over her lips giving them the universal sign to be quiet. "I'm glad you guys could make it." She moved to the phone on the desk and lifted it up, showing the listening device beneath the console. Sophie's eyes widened.

"We won't take up too much of your time. I appreciate you letting us stay so I can learn more about my clairvoyance."

"We're glad we can help. Let me give you a tour of the compound and property and show you where you'll be staying."

"Excellent." Marshall stood and held out his hand for Sophie.

They left the office and Piper started explaining the forty-year-old history of the compound and who the people in the paintings were. There had been six leaders in that time span, each idolized in remembrance.

"We have several classes available. Everything from yoga to meditation, among other more….experimental classes."

"Karma Sutra?" Marshall asked.

"Afraid not." Piper chuckled. "You're at the wrong place for that." She led the way into a huge dining hall filled with several round tables. A long table sat up on a platform in the front of the room. Vases filled with gardenias sat on each table, surrounded by unlit candles.

The strong aroma of coffee filled the air and Sophie grinned. She knew they were probably a holistic bunch, but they still drank coffee, and she only hoped they weren't vegetarians too.

"This is where we gather to eat together." She glanced back at them and continued walking. "You'll be introduced tonight." She continued through a pair of double doors and stepped into a pristine kitchen. Women and men moved around the area, preparing and cooking. Vegetables were being cut. A woman was stirring something in a big pot, and another was trimming fat off of piece of pork. Guess that answered her question. Thank god she wouldn't starve or have to sneak in a double-stacked cheeseburger from town. Having other options besides veggies was going to keep her alive for the next few weeks, depending on how long their investigation lasted.

"Does everyone live on the property?" Sophie asked.

"Some do, however, there are some that just come here to learn about their abilities and don't want to commit. They have day jobs and families so only come when time permits. But a lot of our members wind up staying and helping to support our little community. We have our own greenhouse and gardens on the property. We grow most of our own vegetables and fruits. That not only cuts down on our food costs, but they don't contain any extra additives or fillers." She turned and held out her arms. "We all pitch in to help out. Of course, you're my guests, so you won't be required to do so, but should you decide to call the coven your permanent residence, you'd be required to help."

She turned and pushed through another set of double doors. The blinding sunlight warmed Sophie's face. The fresh air helped settle her nerves and garnered a bit of relief from the ghostly energies she'd had to walk through in the common area.

Piper slid behind the wheel of a four-passenger golf cart and waited for Marshall and Sophie to hop on. Within seconds, they were on a well-travelled dirt path. Piper continued to point out places on the property. The garden, the greenhouse, the fruit trees and crops.

"Some of the couples prefer privacy and live in these." She pointed toward a line of several cottages. They continued up the path toward an outcrop of trees, where a man had a woman pegged up against a tree, and even though they were somewhat shielded, their moans left little to the imagination on what they were doing. "And as you can see, some don't care a thing about privacy."

Piper continued, making several turns and pointing out gazebos where yoga and meditation were held. A few classes were in session.

"This place is bigger than I thought," Sophie announced.

"We even have our own water filtration system and underground bunkers that were installed in the fifties and are still operational."

The dirt path they were on continued past several more buildings before the road started to thin. The outcrop of trees closed in, narrowing and slowing their travel. Sophie kept her arms and legs inside the cart, afraid that she'd be scratched had she not. They'd continued farther down the path before she noticed Marshall's jaw tick. His lips pressed into a fine line.

"We need to walk from here," Piper announced.

They left the cart and continued on foot, stepping over broken limbs and downed trees on the barely visible path that was hardly wide enough for Marshall's body, let alone for them walking in a formation of two.

Piper pushed the overgrown limbs out of the way to open into another clearing. It was a clearing that Sophie recognized and that brought with it an understanding of Marshall's reaction.

"These are the older cabins that are no longer in use. This part of the property is hardly utilized because of how far away it is from the other buildings but I just wanted to make sure you knew they were here."

"We've been here." Marshall slid his fingers though Sophie's. "She was almost killed in that one," he announced with contempt. He jabbed his finger in the direction of the offending little shack sitting off in the distance.

"I'm sorry…. I didn't know."

"It's okay. There's no reason why you should have." Sophie tried to lighten the mood, leaving the memories in the past where they'd be locked away forever.

"Now, do you mind explaining why you have a bug in your office?" Marshall asked accusingly.

"And even more importantly, how you found it. Civilians don't know to look for bugs, much less know what they are when they find them."

Piper clasped her hands in front of her and held Marshall's gaze. "Lucky guess?"

"I don't think so, lady. Start explaining or we walk."

"Let's just say I've had other jobs besides a coven leader. My name is Piper, and my reason for being here is exactly what I told you. My former occupations are the only secrets I've kept. I believe there are more bugs in the building, and there is a lot more going on here than even I can see. These are my people, my friends and my neighbors. I was abandoned as a little girl because of my abilities. My parents called me an abomination, among other things. These people took me in without question. They need my help now, just like I needed theirs. Does that make sense?"

"Yes," Sophie answered for both of them. "It makes perfect sense."

"If you know it's bugged, how come you haven't removed them yet?"

"I haven't decided if I want to use it against whoever is responsible for planting them." She shrugged. "So next time you're in my office, keep that in mind. You won't be able to talk freely."

Marshall pulled out his phone and fired off a text before he shoved the phone away. "Where are we staying?"

"You have your choice of a room in the main building or one of the cottages. I figured it might be easier to pull off being newlyweds if you weren't around prying eyes."

"A cottage is great," Marshall announced, pulling Sophie in front of him and wrapping his arms around her waist. "And just for the record, we won't have a problem pulling off our relationship because we're in one."

Sophie glanced up at him. "We are? How come no one told me?"

Marshall grinned before he tapped her on the ass. "Smartass. Let's go get settled."

They followed behind Piper back toward the foot path that would take them to their ride. Marshall tossed his arm around Sophie's shoulder and his fingers grazed her breast. Talk about a mood changer. Memories of their previous night lingered, his touch welcoming and familiar. She countered with a squeeze to his ass.

They got into the buggy and started the drive back toward civilization.

****

Marshall saw the glint off the gun, poking out from behind the tree, before he heard the gunshot. The loud popping sound of the tire exploding jerked the golf cart, sending it veering off the path and toward the woods. Piper fought the steering wheel to get it back under control. The second pop of a gunshot broke the chaos and sent the entire cart leaning to the left, headed straight toward a steep ravine.

"Jump," Marshall yelled.

Sophie and Marshall jumped from the moving vehicle at the same time. Piper hurled out from the other side. The golf cart disappeared down into a ravine, the crunch of metal their only indication it had stopped.

Marshall grabbed Sophie's hand. His gaze held hers. "Are you okay?"

She nodded and that was the only confirmation he needed, the only reason that the shooter would live to tell the story.

"Are you packing?"

She shook her head. "Not in this dress."

"Shit." He pulled his Glock out of his ankle holster and pointed it into the direction of the trees. He couldn't leave them defenseless and take off after the asshole, but he would fire back to give them needed cover.

"Piper, are you okay?" Sophie yelled.

There was no answer. "Sophie, crawl over and check on her while I cover you. Stay low."

She nodded and didn't hesitate to move. She stayed low, inching against the ground toward where Piper lay.

Marshall scanned the tree line, looking for the glint of a gun, listening for the tiniest tell of where the asshole might be hiding out. All he needed was the crack of a branch, anything to know which direction he needed to shoot.

"How is she?" he hollered.

"She must have hit a rock or something. She's bleeding and unconscious."

Marshall rose from his position and walked backward to where Sophie was kneeling, his eyes still scanning their surroundings. He fired off a warning shot in the direction he'd thought the shots had come from. The noise and the move were designed to draw the bastard out, yet nothing moved. All remained calm. Everything in the woods remained quiet, not even the chirp of a cricket nearby.

He eased down next to Sophie and pointed in the opposite direction of the woods. "You see anything, even an animal, I want you to fire."

She nodded and took the gun out of his hands, covering Marshall. He scooped Piper up into his arms and carried her back over to the path they'd been on. "Anything?"

"Nothing," Sophie answered as her gaze swept the area while walking backward down the path. "We were sitting ducks. Good thing the asshole didn't have great aim."

Marshall shifted Piper's weight for a better hold. "He had excellent aim. He hit those little tires, taking them out while they were in motion."

"Professional?" Sophie asked.

"I'm not sure yet."

Piper's eyes blinked open before they'd made it to the row of cottages. A moan broke her lips. She reached behind her head, her fingers coming away red with her blood. "Ow." She hissed.

"Can you walk?" he asked.

She nodded. "I can try."

He placed her on her feet, keeping his hands on her waist until she steadied. "Switch with me, Sophie."

Sophie handed him the gun and maneuvered her body for Piper to lean on like a crutch to keep her steady.

Marshall didn't put his gun away. That asshole was still out there somewhere. Marshall hadn't heard him move, which meant he was still somewhere in the woods, somewhere watching and maybe even waiting for his next shot.

"Piper, do you normally get hunters on your property?"

She shook her head. "I've heard rumors of them, but not since I've been back. A few used to stray onto our lands, but not lately."

They walked out into the open, his gaze still scanning the woods and the cottages. They were open targets, easy for picking off. He didn't like it one bit. He stuffed the gun beneath his shirt into the waistband of his jeans. If the others saw the weapon, their cover might be blown.

"Do you have an infirmary or are we driving you to the hospital?"

"We have a doctor who lives here. I believe you've already met Nana. If you'll just help me back to the compound, I'll send one of the others to fetch her."

"Where do you want us to stay tonight?" Marshall asked as they rounded the pavilions. Others were starting to stare, unable to hide the questions in their eyes.

"I'd planned to put you up in the old Tanner home. It's the last house on the last row. I was trying to give you some privacy."

He nodded, his gaze still scanning the area and the other residences looking for...what he wasn't sure. A simple smirk on a pair of lips, the glint off a stashed gun. Maybe even someone whispering would tip him off to a new suspect. Yet, he saw nothing but a few glances while they walked the last quarter of a mile into the community center.

The porch was empty upon their return. No one was outside to greet them or offer assistance, but home-cooked smells assaulted his nose. The delightful smell of stew made his stomach growl. Marshall helped ease Piper down onto the nearest sofa. Piper flagged down a passing teenager and sent him to get the doctor. He jogged back out of the building, his face clouded with concern.

Sophie eased around the back of the sofa, brushing her fingers into Piper's hair to part the strands. "It's swollen and scratched, but it's not deep. I don't think she'll need stiches, but she's going to have a headache tomorrow."

"How about we wait to do the introductions tomorrow? That will give you time to rest and time for us to run back into town for additional supplies."

Piper poked at the spot on her head and cringed at the same time Nana came walking through the door, carrying a black medical bag in one hand, using her cane with the other. "What happened? Tommy said you were hurt."

"We had an accident and she hit her head," Marshall said.

"Did you black out?" Nana asked.

"Yes, she did. She was unconscious for about five minutes," Sophie added.

Nana shooed Sophie out of the way and took her spot behind the couch. "I'll take it from here."

Piper nodded. "It's okay. Go do what you need to and we'll meet up in the morning."

She gave them a reassuring smile, a reassurance that meant exactly crap to Marshall. Someone didn't like them being here; it was evident. He knew the risks going under cover, yet Sophie being so close to the action had his nerves on a whole new level. Marshall gripped Sophie's hand in his and walked out the same way they'd arrived. They slid into the SUV, shared a concerned look, and drove back down the dirt path toward the highway.

****

"We're not there thirty minutes and someone took a potshot."

"It means we're on the right track," Marshall replied. "We just need to be more careful. Even I wasn't expecting that."

Sophie feigned her surprise, covering her mouth with her hand. "Not even the great Marshall saw it coming? Whatever will we do?"

He turned to her, a grin stretched across his lips. "I know exactly what we're going to do, but first we're going to get you cleaned up."

She glanced down at the dirt smeared on her dress and tried to wipe it clean.

"Then we're going to get a nice juicy steak because I'm starved. After that, I'm going to make love to you again because you drive me crazy."

"Are we even going to work the case, or was it just a setup so you could spend time with me?"

"Then..." He glanced at her. "We get to work. We're going to be checking for bugs at our new place, and when it gets dark, we'll be setting up surveillance. I already sent a text to the guys to get

43

the register of people who are living there and start background checks on each of them. Dash is having the IT department see if they can dig up anything suspicious. Old records or anything that might give us an idea of what the hell is going on, and I have them getting together some additional equipment we'll need."

"Sounds like you have it all worked out." And it did. Marshall was a smart man. A brilliant, smart, sexy man, and for the next few weeks, she hoped to have him all to herself. She wasn't a naïve woman. Time would tell if he'd end up being possessive like Jack or maybe, even worse, bored with her. Her time was limited, but she'd take what she could get, and right now, her body was begging for his touch, more so than for a full belly.

"Take me to bed and then feed me," she demanded.

"With pleasure."

4 CHAPTER

Sophie sat across from Marshall in the restaurant and watched him polish off the rest of his T-bone steak, her belly and her body sated. He'd even gone above and beyond and ordered them dessert.

"We should be getting back soon."

"Not until I feed you chocolate."

"Smart man." She smiled, ignoring the fluttering butterflies his words gave her.

He grinned around his beer before he took another swig. "All of the equipment is packed. We'll head back when we're done."

The waiter placed a piece of chocolate cake between them before walking away.

She reached for it, pulling it toward her. "You should have ordered your own. You didn't honestly think I'd share, did you?"

He licked his lips. His brows rose in interest. "I may have been hoping for a bite."

She dug her fork in, slicing the cake and bringing the bite up to her lips, making him frown.

She chuckled and reached over, feeding him from her fork. "Just one bite."

Their eyes locked and he held her gaze. His lips wrapped around the fork and she started slowly pulling it out.

Sophie glanced up to find Alexis staring at them with disdain. She was Marshall's ex-girlfriend and Aiden's sister, not to mention a bitch of an attorney Sophie had the displeasure of meeting during her last investigation. Alexis sneered, "Well, isn't this cozy?"

As usual, Alexis's blonde hair was styled to perfection and her black dress hugged her over-exercised curves. The bitch.

Alexis pulled her black wrap tighter around her body. She glanced at Marshall. "You aren't tired of her yet?"

Sophie dropped her fork onto her plate and was about to stand to meet Marshall's ex-girlfriend head-on. The woman he'd dumped to be with Sophie and the same woman who her partner, Aiden, called sister.

"Actually, just the opposite." Marshall reached for her hand and rubbed the diamond ring. "We're married." He glanced up at her. "So, I would appreciate it if you would be nicer to my wife, seeing as how she's not only a partner in the company and you'll be representing us, but your brother's business partner too."

Sophie couldn't take her eyes off Marshall. Her mouth parted before she quickly covered it with a smile. She sat in silence; a bit stunned he'd made the announcement. He smiled and winked before she returned her gaze to Alexis, who was still glaring at both of them. Her eyes narrowed to slits, her face reddened, and her body grew more rigid as she stood even straighter.

"Well." She huffed. "I guess that changes everything."

Alexis ran her finger through Sophie's chocolate cake and then stuck it into her mouth. "I've already had Marshall. I guess it's time to have me some Love." She smirked at Sophie.

"Really? Revenge sex?" Sophie tilted her head. "Now who's the slut?"

"You bitch."

Sophie planted her hands on the table and slowly rose. "You're right about that." She grinned. "Care to see how much worse I can be?"

Alexis narrowed her eyes. "I didn't see your announcement in the paper or I would have sent a gift. I wonder if I'm the only one who doesn't know about this little union. Hmm."

Alexis spun on her heels and walked out of the restaurant without looking back.

"Well, that went better than I would have expected," Marshall announced while Sophie retook her seat.

"Why did you do that?"

"I didn't like the way she was treating you and someone had to put her in her place."

Sophie lowered her head into her hands and took a deep breath before meeting his gaze again. "Do you realize what you've done?"

Marshall leaned back in his chair, tossing one arm on the seatback. He grabbed his beer, his eyes assessing her, his look confused. He took a sip from the bottle. "Why don't you want Jack to know?"

"Because this,"—she wiggled her finger between them both—"isn't real. We aren't married, even if we are dating. You just gave her the ammo she needs to send Jack to blow our cover."

Sophie stood, pulling some bills out of her purse. She dropped them onto the table. "I've lost my appetite. I'll meet you outside."

Sophie walked out. Maybe she was worried about Jack finding out, but it wasn't for the same reason Marshall probably assumed. She liked her cozy little world where she could be herself without a need to explain. Well, that time was over. When Jack got the news that meant her family would also. Marshall started this by kicking a stone over the cliff, not realizing the avalanche he'd just initiated. This called for damage control. Her exhaustion complete, and undeniably seeping into her bones, she leaned back against the SUV.

"This is going to be a long night."

She pulled out her phone and fired off a quick text to Jack. "Heads-up. Marshall and I are playing house in an attempt to catch a killer. We aren't really married, no matter what you hear."

There was a pause before he replied. "Why are you doing this?"

Her fingers flew over the keyboard as she repeated, "To catch a killer."

"That's not what I mean. Why Marshall?"

That question made Sophie pause. She knew all of the reasons in her mind, she knew all the reasons she should say, but only one made sense. The one she wasn't ready to admit. "Because he's the best for the job."

"Sophie, why are you with him?"

"He believes in me. Trusts me and accepts me."

"Love?"

She pondered the question; her fingers paused above the keyboard. "Don't know. Gotta go. We'll talk soon."

She glanced up to see Marshall walking out of the restaurant, carrying a to-go bag. He clicked the fob to unlock the doors. His gaze met hers, but then she broke it and looked back down at her phone.

"Be careful."

His message made her smile. Jack still owned a piece of her heart, and he always would. That would never change. Her friendship with him would never change, even if that meant she was in an awkward position. She liked Marshall. More than that, she liked how she felt when she was around him. His actions and his words make her feel competent and strong. It was a new feeling, liberating.

He stopped in front of her and held up the bag. "I'm sorry."

She took the bag and peeked inside. Three containers of different desserts were inside. The tension in her shoulders eased. She'd confessed to

49

Jack, now it was Marshall's turn to handle the rest. Her aggravation was forgotten.

"You're forgiven. While you were buying out their dessert cart, I was fixing our problem." She held up her phone before stuffing it back in her purse. "I sent a text to Jack."

"Crises averted," he announced, stepping closer to her. His body pressed against hers. He palmed her cheek and held her gaze. "I'm not sorry I told Alexis. I'm sorry I made you worry about Jack."

Sophie slid her palm up Marshall's chest and around to cup his neck. "Silly man. I wasn't worried about Jack knowing. I was worried about his reaction." She tilted her head. "There's a difference."

He pressed his body into hers, pushing her back against the SUV. His hands on her cheeks, he claimed her lips with the same amount of fierce passion she'd seen in his eyes the first time they'd made love. His tongue tangled with hers and she relaxed into the moment. Every nerve in her body strained to be closer, strained for his touch to sate her needs.

He slowed the kiss until he eventually pulled back. "I guess we need to tell your brother next."

She grinned. "You get the honor of that one."

"Chicken?"

"He's always expected to have a say in the man I marry. He wanted to threaten him and put the fear of God in him, like any good big brother would. I'm betting he's going to feel slighted you stole his glory." She raised her brow, opened the door, and slid inside the SUV. Before closing it, she couldn't contain her grin. "Good luck with that."

Sophie chuckled to herself while watching Marshall make his way around the SUV. His look was determined. He was mumbling beneath his breath. He slid inside. "I guess we have one more stop to make."

Sophie smiled and kept to herself until they pulled into Max and Eileen's driveway. Sophie took her bag of goodies with her. Max met them at the door. Sophie kissed his cheek and sidestepped him into the house and headed straight for the kitchen. She grabbed two forks and walked back into the living room to find Eileen reading a book. Sophie nudged her, plopping down on the couch beside her.

"What are you doing here?"

"I brought the after-dinner entertainment," Sophie answered while pulling out one of the containers and handing the lemon cake to her sister-in-law, along with a fork.

Eileen's mouth parted, but she just shrugged. "Okay."

Sophie kicked off her shoes and crossed her legs beneath her. She brought new meaning to the words bad wife. "The show is about to begin."

Max walked into the living room with Marshall bringing up the rear. He met Sophie's gaze. There was a faint glint of humor in his eyes.

"What are you doing here?" Max asked, stopping in front of the coffee table, his curious gaze watching Sophie and Eileen.

"Ask him," Sophie answered with a motion toward Marshall with her fork.

Max folded his arms over his chest and turned to face Sophie's fake husband. "Well?"

"Sophie and I are under cover."

"Okay," Max answered. "If you're under cover, then why are you here?"

"To show you this." Sophie held up her hand and wiggled her wedding ring.

Eileen's fork dropped into her container. She tossed the dessert aside and grabbed Sophie's hand, yanking her closer. "What? *When*?"

Max's nostrils flared and his hands fisted by his sides. He grabbed Marshall and spun him around to face him. "What the hell did you do?"

Sophie chuckled. "It's not what you think."

"Well, are you married or not?" her brother demanded.

"It depends on who you ask." Marshall shrugged. "For the sake of our cover, we are a newly and very happily married couple. As far as the state goes, our union might or might not be recognized in a court of law."

"So I don't have to kick your ass?" Max asked Marshall.

"Afraid not this time, but don't worry, when I do talk her into marrying me for real, you'll be the first to know, and then you can try."

"Wha...."

"Surprise," Sophie announced, cutting in to turn the attention away from what Marshall had announced. She was unable to hide the amusement from her face. "And we had to tell Love before Alexis mentioned it, so he might be cranky for a while at work."

"What the hell did you do?" Max asked, ignoring Marshall's previous statement. The fight previously displayed evaporated in a big exhale from his body. He plopped down in his recliner. "Which case are you working?" he asked, glancing from her to Marshall. "It better not be the Pentagram."

"It is," Sophie answered and rose from her spot. She placed her container down and confronted her brother head-on. "And I don't want to hear any reason why I can't do this. I am doing this. It's already a done deal, and now we have to leave."

Sophie took her fork back into the kitchen and rinsed it off in the sink. Her brother followed, leaving Marshall and Eileen in the living room. "Do you really think this is a good idea?"

"Yeah." She turned off the water and dried her hands. "I do. The killer is already taking the bait. We got shot at today in the woods."

"You what!"

She patted his chest. "Don't worry. Marshall had his weapon. We just came back in town for some gear." She reached up and kissed his cheek. "I love you; don't worry. Okay?"

"No, not okay."

"Well, we have to go. I'll check in after we're settled, in a few days. Hold down the fort, and if you get a chance, can you keep an eye on my house? Don't worry. I don't need you to water any plants. I don't own any because I can't keep the damn things alive. "

"This is a bad idea," he argued.

Marshall ambled into the kitchen, tossed his arm around her shoulders, and pulled her into his side. "I'll take care of her, Max. Not that she needs my help, but I'll do what's necessary to keep her safe."

Max's gaze followed Marshall's arm. His face twisted; his nod of approval was fleeting. "Cripes...are you two..."

"Dating?" she supplied. "Yes, yes we are."

"What happened to Love?"

Eileen walked into the kitchen and rubbed her husband's back. "I'll explain everything later, sweetie. We should let them get on the road."

Sophie and Marshall said their goodbyes and were in the SUV five minutes later. The vehicle's lights shone on the pavement, illuminating the dark road. The drive back to the compound seemed longer than before.

The moon was high in the night sky, her body tired. All she wanted was a comfortable bed and a good night's sleep.

"Well, that wasn't so bad."

"That's because I saved you. I should have made you tell him." She rested her head against the leather seat and turned her gaze toward him.

"I will, if you ever accept my real proposal. I'll do it right next time, now that I know."

Sophie ignored the comment. "What do we have to do when we get back? Is sleep even on the agenda?"

He glanced at her before reaching for her hand. He threaded his fingers with hers. "Are you tired?"

She nodded and tried to stifle her yawn. "Extremely."

Marshall rubbed his finger over the top of her palm. "You can get some sleep. I'll take care of the rest."

"Thanks, baby."

****

Marshall pulled up outside their assigned cottage and killed the ignition on the SUV. He glanced in her direction. Her sleeping body leaned back in the seat, her head turned toward the side. Her fingers had loosened against his ten minutes into the drive.

He got out and walked around to her side. He eased her door open, intent on carrying her across the threshold. She blinked her eyes open. "Are we here?"

"We are." He helped her out. "Let's get you into bed and I'll come back for the bags."

He moved to shut the door and she stopped him. She reached back in for the desserts and her purse. "I can't leave these."

He grinned. "It's true what they say; a way to a girl's heart is through dessert."

"You're learning, Dixon."

"Yes, I am, Mrs. Dixon."

"Do you need me to help with whatever we have left to do?" she asked around her yawn.

Marshall turned the knob on the door and pushed it open with mixed feelings of gratitude and concern that he hadn't needed a key. His night was getting longer by the minute. His job tonight would be thorough.

"No, Sophie. I'll take care of it as soon as I check for any unwanted guests."

They walked in and flicked on the lights. What looked rustic and small on the outside was clean and bigger on the inside. The smell of cleaning supplies assaulted his nose. A fire flickered in the fireplace with extra wood sitting nearby. They moved farther inside toward the breakfast bar. A bottle of champagne was chilling in the silver bucket with a note sitting next to it. Sophie picked it up and flipped it open. She smiled and turned back to him. "Aw...that was sweet. They left us a welcome gift."

"We aren't drinking that. It could be drugged."

"Spoilsport."

"I'll have the good stuff delivered tomorrow, and it probably wouldn't hurt to stock our little kitchen so we don't have to eat with them every night we're here."

He took her hand and guided her down the short hallway, opening doors as he went. The one bedroom, one-and-a-half-bath house was a bit cramped, but it would work for the time being, and it was a better option than being in the main building.

He pulled back the covers and helped her take off her shoes and her jeans. He waited for her to slide beneath the covers before pressing a kiss to her smiling lips. "Thank you, husband."

He paused before straightening. "Are you testing it out?"

"I guess you could say that I'm taking it for a test drive."

He chuckled. "Good night, my sweet wife."

"I'm not sweet," she mumbled and rolled into the covers, their banter over.

He eased out of the room, flicking the light off behind him. His goals included bringing in their supplies, scanning the rooms for listening devices, and setting up a makeshift alarm, all before his head would hit the pillow tonight.

The older hardwood floors creaked in some areas he walked over. The appliances in the kitchen were old. What had looked nice upon arriving, after further inspection, wasn't up to his particular standards. White panel walls doubled as drywall, the slats muted tan and aged from time. He backed the SUV up to the front door planning an easy escape and a quicker unloading of their supplies and clothes. He dropped everything in the living room before he locked it all up. He took out the electronic equipment, scanning and listening to the squeals, and located several listening devices. He found one beneath a vase, another inside the lamp shade, even more around the phones and throughout the kitchen, and several stashed beneath the furniture. Someone was going to be pissed the next time they tried to listen in. Either way, they'd find the culprit when they came to recheck the equipment or came asking questions. Regardless, getting rid of the equipment was necessary to their investigation.

He tackled the vents next, checking those and everything in the cabin to make sure there were no video feeds coming or going. Luckily for them, whoever had bugged the place hadn't thought that far ahead.

He took out another tiny piece of equipment, flicked the switch and grinned. Until he had more time and energy to explore, the continuous electronic pulsing device would disable anything within their walls that he may have missed.

Marshall took a beer out of the cooler they'd brought and popped the top. He eased down on the couch in front of the fire. The crackle of the wood could easily lull him into a false feeling of safety. Their new home was devoid of a television and it was probably a good thing. They needed to concentrate on catching the asshole that had shot at them, not get relaxed enough to watch a football game.

Marshall glanced around the small space, his eyes trained to search the area for entry points and exits. They would need a route out and a backup plan to escape. He still had to set up some type of security around the perimeter and in the house and transmit the video feed back to the IT department to watch in the event someone tried to break in when neither Sophie nor him were home.

He took another sip of his beer, letting the cool liquid slide down his throat. He pulled his phone out of his pocket to check his email. He deleted one from Alexis without reading it and answered a few of his work emails. Running on reserves, he finally decided to call it a night. He locked the door, changed into his night clothes, and stashed guns within his reach and hers, including one beneath his pillow. He eased into the bed and pulled her body close to his. He needed her warmth; he needed her strength; and if he was honest, he needed her.

Sleep didn't come easy. Every creak in the old house got checked. The single-paned windows did little to muffle the sounds of crickets, frogs, and an occasional howl outside. His sleep would be minimal until he had some type of security in place, something to warn when things went bump in the night.

****

Sophie rolled on the bed, looking for her fake husband to snuggle with. She stole his pillow, inhaling his familiar scent. Her fingers stroked the gun beneath. She smiled and sat up. She glanced around the unfamiliar room, bringing her back to the real reason they were together. The real reason why they were in the unfamiliar house. The room was small and homey, sparse to the eye and severely lacking in color and personification.

Sophie inhaled again and the aroma of coffee drifted to her nose. The smell had her on her feet and throwing on a pair of yoga pants from her bag. She gathered her hair and twisted it in a ponytail before making her way out of the room. The first order of the day was a shower and coffee, and not necessarily in that order.

She left the room and rounded the corner into the kitchen. Marshall leaned against the counter, sipping a cup of coffee.

"Good morning, sunshine."

She grinned and picked up the mug he'd already poured for her. She took a long sip, letting the smell waft through her, her eyes closed in bliss. "It is now."

Sophie sat on one of the bar stools and picked up one of the little black objects that had been grouped together. "What are these?"

"Someone wanted to eavesdrop."

"Again?" She shook her head and took another sip of her coffee, remembering the last dead asshole that had rigged her house with video and devices. The same dead asshole that had yet to show up in the afterlife to pay her a visit. "Did you check the bathrooms?"

"Of course." He grinned. "I removed theirs and put in my own."

She winked and patted his chest. "That's my husband. Always thinking ahead. Next you'll want to make a sex tape."

He chuckled. "I didn't know that was an option."

She glanced over her shoulder and winked. "We could arrange something, if you're a good boy."

Sophie walked down the hall toward the bathroom, stopping at every loose board that creaked. She bounced on the balls of her feet. The creaking wood might serve as a warning system.

"I'm afraid one of these boards is going to break. How old is this house anyway?" She stepped into the bedroom and grabbed a change of clothes and her toiletries before moving into the bathroom.

"My guess is around forty years old. I'm surprised we don't have ghosts," Marshall answered through the closed door.

"Knock on wood," she replied.

"That won't be a problem. These walls are painted wood panels." He leaned over on the bed and knocked on the wall. "You need any help in there?"

Sophie turned on the shower, ditched her clothes and stepped under the warm spray. "Nope. If you come in, we'll never meet the neighbors."

"It is our honeymoon. I'm sure they aren't expecting to see us until lunch."

"More of a reason to hit them early. They won't see it coming. Maybe we can catch a few of them gossiping."

Marshall set his mug down on the bedside table and leaned back on the unmade bed. "All work and no play makes you boring."

The shower turned off minutes later and she opened the door in her birthday suit. "Be a good boy and we'll call it an early night." She winked and shut the door again to get dressed. Emerging fifteen minutes later in a pair of jeans and a royal blue tank top, she twisted her hair up into another ponytail, refusing to dry it. After touring the compound, there weren't many women wearing the traditional dresses, so neither did she. She'd chosen the girl-next-door makeup to go along with the less-is-more theme the compound had adopted.

She grabbed his hand and placed a kiss on his cheek. "Let's go stir-up the natives and see who bites first."

"I like the way you think, Mrs. Dixon."

5 CHAPTER

"I'll remind you that you said that the next time we get shot at."

He pulled her to a stop before they made it out the door. "Where's your gun?"

She rolled her eyes. "In my purse. No one is going to attack today in broad daylight with witnesses."

"They did yesterday."

"Good point." She walked over to her purse and tossed the strap over her head and across her body.

They left the house holding hands. Their street was busy with adults and workers as they went about their day. A few older people sat on the porch; one sewing and another working what looked to be a crossword puzzle. A group of women were sitting Indian-style on blankets. Their palms rested face up on their thighs and their eyes were closed as they meditated. Another group was in the gazebo practicing some form of yoga that had them bending over with their butts up in the air. Sophie grinned.

"You know you want to try that," Marshall teased while lacing his fingers through hers.

"I bet you'd love to see my ass up in the air," she countered.

He wiggled his brows. The closer they got to the main dining hall, the louder her stomach growled in anticipation.

"Let's hope they have bacon," she whispered and opened the door to the dining hall. They bypassed the common area where a few people sat talking while nursing glasses filled with green goop. They sipped and talked, and all Sophie could think about was the grass they were digesting. Her stomach rolled in displeasure.

"Let's get you one of those," Marshall whispered.

"Let's not." Sophie patted her husband's stomach.

They stepped into the dining hall and stopped. The room was only half full. About thirty men and woman total sat at the various tables, including the old woman, Nana. She was sitting with Piper and another guy.

Piper waved them over and Sophie led the way. Marshall pulled out her chair and then took a seat next to her.

"How are you feeling?" Marshall asked.

"Better." Piper replied. "Sophie, Marshall, I know you met Nana yesterday, but this is her nephew, Franklin."

"Hi," Sophie greeted him.

"Hmm," he replied in a grunt.

"He doesn't talk much," Piper acknowledged. "He's one of the woodsmen in our commune. All of the fireplace wood is compliments of him."

"So he's good with an axe," Sophie acknowledged. "That's good to know." She grinned. "And thanks for the heat."

"Hmm," he grunted again, only this time with a nod.

Another man walked up to the table and sat down next to Piper. "This is Kevin. He's Nana's other nephew. If you've got something broken, he's the guy to go to. He can fix anything."

"Hi," Sophie greeted him, hoping that maybe this one might talk more than his brother.

"Hi." He tilted his head toward the kitchen. "If you two are going to eat, I'd suggest you hurry. They're closing the kitchen in ten minutes."

Marshall rose and leaned over, kissing her cheek. "I'll get you a plate, baby. Why don't you just relax?"

She looked up at him and grinned. "Thanks, honey."

"You been married long?" Kevin asked.

"Seems like it was just yesterday. We're still newlyweds."

"That's nice." Kevin smiled. "If you guys are interested, I also teach yoga and a few more things you'll find on the calendar."

"Great. We're just feeling our way around right now, but I'm sure we'll start participating. It's the reason we're here."

"So, what's your specialty?" he asked. "Are you a medium, clairvoyant, psychic, witch, or just someone interested in our kind?"

"Well, I don't like labels, but I guess you could say I'm clear seeing, clear knowing, and I also do some remote viewing,"—she grinned—"on their territory."

His mouth parted. "Clairvoyant, claircognizant, and you can remote view to the other side?"

"That's the best way to describe it when they yank me away, regardless of whether or not I want to go."

Kevin moved his chair closer to her. "What's that like, and why wouldn't you want to go?" He rested his chin in his hand, his food forgotten. "That has to be amazing."

Marshall walked out of the kitchen, carrying two plates. She met his gaze and watched the confusion on his face as if trying to figure out why Kevin had moved closer and was practically sitting in her lap.

"Did you replace me already?" Marshall set her plate down in front of her and took his seat beside her.

"Well, you *were* gone five minutes. It could happen."

Kevin straightened in his chair. "I wasn't encroaching. Sophie was just telling us about her abilities. I've never heard of being yanked to the other side. That's amazing."

Marshall rubbed Sophie's back. "I knew she was special the first day I met her. It took me a little bit longer to get her to say yes."

"That's so sweet," Piper replied. "Well, if you'll excuse us, we'll let you eat in peace."

They all rose and picked up their dishes. "We're on dish and kitchen duty."

Nana squeezed Sophie's shoulder in passing. "See what you have to look forward to? You guys let me know if you need anything."

Sophie chanced a glance at Marshall before meeting Nana's gaze. "Thanks. We appreciate that."

Sophie watched everyone leave before she even picked up her fork. Eggs, fruit and some type of grits were on her plate. Her mouth parted and she looked up. "You don't love me?"

He chuckled. "They were out of the good stuff. I was told if you snooze, you lose." He shrugged. "Maybe we should just plan on eating breakfast in our shack. That way I can make sure you get all the meat you need."

"Oh, that sounds like the best plan you've had yet, but it's counterproductive to our plans." She glanced around the almost empty room. A few stragglers were pushing out the door. "Maybe we should discuss our future plans when we get back. You know.....in case you'd rather others know about your affinity of feeding me meat and wanting me to learn yoga."

Marshall's brow rose and he grinned. He picked up a pen from a nearby table and started scribbling on a napkin. *Visually, I've noticed three bugs already. I think this whole place is infected.*

67

She smiled after reading the note. "We'll have to discuss what, exactly, to do about that."

He nodded. "I've got a few ideas on how to make that happen." He winked.

He used his fork and gestured toward her plate. "Why don't you eat before it gets cold and then we'll take a walk? Maybe meet some of the others."

She reached over and rubbed his arm. "You're the best hubby ever." She chuckled before shoving a bite of watermelon into her mouth.

They both finished eating, staying away from the weird smelling grits. They each took their plates into the already empty kitchen and cleaned them. Even though they were guests on this property, they'd leave it just the way they'd found it.

Sophie wrapped her palm around Marshall's arm, guiding him toward the back door. The golf cart from the day before was sitting outside, the frame beaten and dimpled and two of the four tires sat flat. Marshall squatted next to the vehicle and ran his hand around the outside of the tire. He pressed his finger into the hole.

"We were lucky."

"I wouldn't call getting shot at lucky," Marshall replied.

"We didn't get hit." She glanced around them to make sure there weren't any prying eyes or ears she could see before she leaned down next to him. "Max will want forensics to exam the cart to see if the bullets are still lodged inside. They might match the ballistics to another killing."

"I'll have to work some magic to make it disappear for a while."

"I'm sure Piper won't mind."

Sophie rose and held out her hand. "Let's go see what else we can get into."

He stood and rubbed the stubble on his chin, his gaze still on the wheels.

She wrapped her palm around his arm and tugged him in the direction she wanted to go. "Was there any DNA left at the scenes?"

"I've read the reports. There was very little the killer left behind. From what they could tell, ropes and duct tape used were from each victim's house."

"How about we don't buy any ropes for our shack." She grinned. "The killer won't have anything to tie us up with."

Marshall snapped his fingers. "Shucks. Then I won't have anything to tie you to the bed."

"You can use your ties." She winked.

"I didn't pack any, but I'm sure we'll figure something out."

Sophie walked up to the pavilion where they'd been doing yoga. The original people were gone, replaced with different people who were in the process of meditating. Music filled the pavilion. A slow hum and the ringing of bells drifted to her ears. Marshall leaned into her. "Go make friends."

She grinned. "Are you trying to get rid of me already?"

He shook his head. "I know how important it is for you to meet others like you, not to mention the other reasons we're here." He guided her toward the entrance. "I'll be back at our place. I still have a few things to check on, but I'll be waiting when you get back."

Sophie smiled; her heart full. She did want to meet others like her. With her work and home life, she might not find time to take advantage of another opportunity like this one. She kissed him before patting his ass. "I'm glad you're my husband. I'm a lucky girl."

She walked away and into the pavilion, only glancing back once to find Marshall watching her. His gaze met hers, piercing her heart. She'd left him speechless. Just the way he belonged.

Sophie eased down into an open spot amid the group. She kicked off her shoes and crossed her legs. She glanced toward where Marshall stood once more before turning straight and closing her eyes. She concentrated on her breathing, letting the tensions float from her body. Lights flickered behind her lids, the sound of the music soothing, opening her chakras and lulling her into a deeper state.

Will's face popped in her mind, his voice in her ear. "It's about time."

She smiled and opened her eyes to find that she was no longer in the pavilion but in a field near a lake. There was a group sitting around a log with a fire, similar in style to the way she was sitting in the pavilion. The only difference was that these weren't the same people. These people were different. Will stood between her and them and started walking her way.

He took Sophie by the elbow and led her in the other direction, away from the spirits sitting by the fire.

"Who are they?" she asked.

"They're not your concern."

She twisted her elbow out of his grasp. "Why are you being evasive?"

His lips curled. "You wouldn't know how to deal with me if I wasn't."

Sophie couldn't help but roll her eyes.

The scene around them changed. The people in the field were gone, along with the lake. This time they were in a room that resembled Sophie's living room. There was a familiar feel, although something was just a bit off. Something she couldn't put her finger on. Sophie walked around the room, looking to pinpoint exactly what was different.

"Why are we here?"

Will shrugged. "I thought you'd be more comfortable."

Sophie eased down onto her couch, tucking her legs beneath her. "I suppose you don't want to give me the name of the killer."

"No," Will answered, sitting on the edge of her coffee table. "You need to meditate more."

"Maybe I would, if you answered more questions," she countered.

"You still have a lot to learn. Your abilities will continue to grow."

"I know." Her voice came out as a whisper, and she slowly nodded. "I'm not sure what else there is to know, but I can feel that I've just skimmed the surface."

"Enlightenment, love, acceptance and guidance….you have so much to offer, and yet you refuse."

"I don't refuse," she said. "I'm just finding a different path, one that I'm comfortable with."

"You need to start trusting yourself and your instincts."

"I already do," Sophie answered, confused as to where Will was headed with his comments.

"Do you remember what I said about this case?" he asked.

She nodded. "Yeah, you told me, during my last case, that I would be hurt on my next one."

He nodded and his lips turned down into a frown. "I'm sorry."

A scream rent the air, making Sophie's eyes pop open. She glanced around her. Everyone who had been in her group was nowhere to be found. A woman about the same age as Sophie stood near the entrance with a yoga mat in her arms. The newcomer's brown eyes were wide with fear. She pointed to the middle of the floor. A long snake was curled, its head in the air, and swaying as if he was ready to strike.

"Don't move," the woman exclaimed.

Sophie's heart raced, her gaze fixed. How the hell had she let this happen and what had happened to the others? The speakers for the music were gone, and the sun was setting. She was disoriented. When she'd been with Will, it had seemed mere minutes, but under the circumstances, it must have been several hours since she'd sat down.

The snake lifted its tale into the air. The rattling noise it made chilled her to the bone. Her hands trembled as she pressed them against the wood, ready to rise and run, praying that her attempt wouldn't fail.

Sophie eased her hand over to her purse. Her gun was the only option she had; when in reality, a shovel would have worked better or any type of protection other than of the bullet kind.

"I'll try and distract it, giving you a chance to run," the woman announced.

She unfolded her mat and held it in front of her as the snake now swayed back and forth between both women. The lady with the mat eased toward the entrance.

"What if I throw my mat on him?"

Sophie shook her head. "Then you won't be protected if he turns on you."

Sophie caught movement on her right, opposite of where the woman stood. The woodsman, she'd met in the cafeteria, stood there with an axe in hand.

"Winnie, go get Nana," Franklin demanded, his voice sure and deep. "Mrs. Dixon, I need you to remain very still."

"You don't have to worry about that." Sophie sat motionless; the only movements in her body were the rapid beating of her heart and the blood rushing to her ears.

Marshall appeared at the other entrance. His gaze went from Sophie to the snake and back. His eyes were wide, his hand going for his waistband. Before he could pull his gun, Franklin threw his axe.

The lumberjack's blade sliced through the air cutting the snake's head from his body before the weapon impaled against the far wall of the wooden structure. The tail dropped to the ground. Sophie fell backward, closed her eyes, and let out a breath she didn't realize she'd been holding. She rested her hand on her chest trying to calm her heart and stave off a potential heart attack.

Nature was not her friend. Her idea of roughing it was walking to the coffee shop without having caffeine first.

Sophie opened her eyes. Marshall kneeled beside her, his hands running down her arms and legs. "Did you get bit?"

She shook her head. "No."

"Why didn't you leave with the others?" Marshall asked.

Franklin yanked his axe out of the wood and walked over the dead snake. He slammed the axe down again. Picking up the snake's tail, he set the rattler next to Sophie. "Souvenir."

"You shouldn't have." She glanced up at Franklin. "Really."

Marshall rose, holding out his hand to help her off the ground. Nana's cane thudded against the wood with each step as she moved into the pavilion with her medical bag in her hand.

"Sorry, false alarm," Sophie announced.

"Are you okay, child?" Nana asked.

"Yes. Franklin showed up just in time and slayed the beast."

Franklin walked out of the pavilion and disappeared into the trees.

"We have all kinds of animals out here. You might want to consider carrying a knife."

She nodded. "I was just thinking the same thing."

Marshall slid his fingers through Sophie's and stepped down out of the pavilion.

"You forgot your rattle," Nana announced.

Sophie wrinkled her nose. "Not something I care to remember." A shiver skirted down her spine. The rattler was a silent reminder of how close she'd come to death. Again.

Silently, Marshall led her away from the pavilion heading toward the last row of houses.

"I'm sorry," Sophie announced. "I must have been under pretty good to not hear the others leave."

He glanced at her, his brows creased. Yet he remained silent until he had her inside the house with the door closed.

"No more meditation, not unless I'm with you."

Sophie's mouth parted. "I was with several others."

"Your eyes were closed and you were vulnerable. You almost died."

Sophie couldn't argue that. All of his statements were true, regardless of whether or not she liked it. "How do you suppose I meditate to meet with Will?"

"Here." Marshall stalked farther into the living room and turned around to face her. "You're safe in here."

Sophie walked over to Marshall and slid her palms up his chest to clasp her fingers behind his neck. "If I don't socialize, we'll never find our answers."

Marshall folded his arms across his chest, a move that Sophie didn't see often. "Not at the cost of your life. Thank god Paul Bunyan was there."

Sophie grinned. "Good thing he knows how to wield an axe."

Marshall's lips tilted at the corner. "This isn't funny, Sophie."

"I know, but think about it for just a minute, Marshall. That snake probably just slithered into the wrong place at the right time. I'm sure someone didn't plant him there. What if I'd come out of meditation sooner. I would have caught them in the act."

Marshall pulled Sophie into his warm embrace and kissed the top of her head. "I almost lost you."

"But you didn't." She leaned back and her gaze met his. "Come to think of it, why was Franklin there?"

"Maybe he'd reached his quota of scared animals in the forest."

One look at the big guy and most people, let alone animals, would be running the other way. Franklin was a big guy. He didn't have a five o'clock shadow; he had a midnight bush on his chin. His presence was dangerous and scary, the axe not helping to soften his image. Standing at least six feet five inches tall, the guy towered over the others. He was wearing the same type of attire earlier that morning. Flannel shirts and jeans must be the standard outfit for trampling through the woods to make all of the bunnies scared.

"I bet he's a big teddy bear under that ox-like exterior." Sophie stepped out of Marshall's embrace, walked into the kitchen, and grabbed a bottle of water from the fridge.

"I'll bet you twenty bucks you're wrong and he's our guy."

Sophie paused with the water bottle halfway to her mouth. Was he joking? "You're on. As a matter of fact, I'll raise your twenty to a hundred bucks."

He eased up to her and leaned against the counter, a grin spreading across his face. "I'll raise your hundred to a simple yes. If I'm right, you marry me….for real."

"And if you're wrong?"

He shrugged. "You're already a partner. What do you want?"

Sophie touched her tongue to her top lip. "Let me think about it." She winked. "I'll get back to you on that one."

He glanced at his watch. "We've got to go, or we're going to be late for our introduction dinner."

Sophie grabbed her purse and tossed the strap over her head to drape across her body. She pulled the door open and waited for him to grab his gun. "What's on the menu tonight?"

"You."

"Well, that's a given. I'm talking about food, husband. Don't make me hurt you."

Marshall flicked a few switches before pulling their cabin door closed. "I like the sound of that."

"Me hurting you?" Sophie slid her hand into Marshall's and started walking back down the street toward the common area. "I didn't know you were into that, but I can give it a try."

"No, I like hearing you call me husband."

"It's temporary." She nudged his shoulder.

"When that's gone, so is the sex." He nudged her back.

She poked out her bottom lip but didn't give him a spicy retort. In her gut she knew when this was over things were bound to change. There was no denying the line they'd crossed or what would happen next.

They were just about at the common area when Piper emerged from the side of the building. She motioned them over, her gaze darting around the area and behind her. She ushered them to the side of the building.

"You guys are in trouble, and there is nothing I can do to stop it," Piper said in a whisper with urgency in her tone. "You guys need to leave."

6 CHAPTER

"You know we can't," Sophie answered. She placed her palm on Piper's arm to get the woman's attention. "What's wrong?"

Piper rubbed at her temples, her eyes squeezing shut before she opened them. "This place is following old rituals. You have to believe me; I didn't know. I thought they quit doing it a year after I left."

"What are you talking about?" Marshall asked.

"There's a ceremony. Everyone who's married is expected to attend." Piper's gaze moved quickly between Sophie and Marshall. "It's a vow renewal. Love and commitment is a prominent part for each couple in learning to accept a person's new abilities."

The lines on Marshall's face softened. "That sounds pretty easy. I thought you were going to say they were sacrificing a virgin or something."

"You don't understand." Piper's eyes widened. "It's performed by an ordained minister. You two will legally be married if you participate."

Sophie's head started shaking back and forth, even though no words were coming out of her mouth.

Marshall started laughing though Sophie was panicking. She slapped his abs. "This isn't funny."

"It kind of is," he answered.

"How do we get out of it?" Sophie asked Piper.

Piper tilted her head as if trying to figure out what Marshall found so humorous in the situation and it was something Sophie didn't want to try to explain.

"You can't," she answered. "It's scheduled for three days from now. If you guys haven't solved the case, then as a married couple, you'll be forced to participate. Otherwise, it will make people suspicious."

Marshall moved to stand behind Sophie and started rubbing her shoulders. "We've handled worse. Everything will be okay."

Sophie took a deep breath and nodded. "It just means we'll have to work double time or come up with a reason not to attend."

Marshall's hands slowed on her shoulders. "You're right. Come on, love bunny. Let's go mingle and make some friends."

"Love bunny?" Sophie questioned.

"What? Don't you like it?"

Sophie was quick to answer. "Uh…no."

"Sugar butt?" Marshall asked.

"Maybe if you're from another world and carry a big hammer, and even then, I don't think he'd use the words sugar butt."

"I've got a big hammer for you, baby," Marshall whispered into Sophie's ear as they entered the building.

Piper led the way to a long table that had been set up on a platform along the wall. All the seats were already full. She gestured to a table in front of the podium, motioning for them to sit, before she took her rightful spot up on the makeshift stage. Food was served and glasses filled. Piper stood up, tapping her spoon against her water glass.

The noise in the room tapered off and Piper cleared her throat. "I'm sure many of you have noticed that we have two new guests on the property. I'd like to take a moment to welcome Sophie and Marshall Dixon, our new honeymooners. Some of you may have seen them around town, but Sophie has just recently come into her own abilities and is curious about our coven. Please give her and Marshall a warm welcome."

A round of applause sounded throughout the room, along with a few hoots and hollers. Sophie felt the blush creeping up her neck.

"I'm Ted, your neighbor," the man sitting next to Sophie announced.

"I'm Winnie." The woman reached across Ted's plate to shake Sophie's hand. "We haven't officially met, but I saw you at the pavilion. I live in the apartment upstairs."

Winnie had taken her hair out of the ponytail. Her brown hair was styled straight and reached down her back to her waist. She looked different than when Sophie had seen Winnie the first time, or maybe it was just due to the adrenaline from the snake that she hadn't noticed how pretty Winnie really was. Her face was flawless, with only a hint of makeup accentuating her features, and her smile was bright.

"Hi," Sophie replied while picking up her fork. She poked around at the mashed potatoes, wondering if they were truly mashed potatoes or maybe a rendition of something else all mashed up. She watched Marshall take a tentative bite of his. He gave a slight nod, confirming that it was a vegetable that she'd recognize. She took a bite, surprised that the potatoes were actually pretty tasty, even if they weren't smothered in butter or gravy. No toppings were a new concept, not one that she'd take home with her, but at least the lumps were edible.

"I don't know how you stayed so still at the pavilion. That snake could have killed you."

"I was lucky Franklin showed up."

Winnie nodded in agreement.

"I hear someone shot at you, too," Ted said, making Sophie almost choke on her potatoes.

"I heard it was a poacher," Winnie explained.

Sophie shared a quick look at Marshall.

"Do those types of accidents happen around here often?" Marshall asked.

"Oh no, never," Winnie replied. "We haven't had any crime here in ten years."

Sophie tilted her head, not sure what to make of the woman. Was she smoking something? Maybe had a glass of wine before she'd come to dinner? "What about Mary?"

"She wasn't the victim of a crime," Ted announced. "She died from natural causes."

Sophie paused mid bite and eased her hand back down. "Is that so?"

"Sure," Winnie replied. "Piper said it was a heart attack."

Sophie glanced over her shoulder at the woman who'd asked them to come investigate. Why the lie? Was it to keep everyone calm? Didn't these people deserve to know they had a killer among them?

"Do you guys get the newspaper out here?" Sophie asked as she turned back around, exchanging a quick confused glance with Marshall. Sophie had read the article about Mary's death and how the police were investigating the crime. Why hadn't these people?

"Sure we do." Winnie tilted her head as if trying to remember something. "But come to think of it, I haven't seen one in the last month." She glanced at Ted who just shrugged his shoulders. "I'll have to mention that to Piper."

"Are there a lot of snakes around here?" Marshall asked changing the subject.

"Yep," Ted answered. "You need to watch out for the scorpions and spiders too. Every morning, I check my boots before I put them on. I suggest you do the same."

Sophie's eyes widened as a shiver skirted down her spine. Her feet felt more exposed in the flip-flops she had on.

"Have you two been in the coven long?" Sophie asked, trying desperately to ignore her feet.

"I've been here two years," Winnie announced. "Ted has been here ten."

"So you both are familiar with the property?" Marshall asked.

"Oh yeah. We're our own little family out here. Everyone is super helpful. If you get lost, just ask any one of them. They'll point you in the right direction."

Sophie took a sip of her water. Her appetite diminished along with the thought of something crawling on her toes. "I hear there's a vote coming up pretty soon for Mary's replacement. Are either of you considering the position?"

They exchanged a glance before Winnie leaned closer. "It doesn't work like that around here. It's supposed to, but it doesn't."

"Oh?" Sophie asked, trying hard not to show her confusion.

"In the other covens, it's a democracy." Winnie announced. "Here it's more like a dictatorship. The votes don't really count. It's whoever is next in line. The heir from the oldest family here is put into the position. Kind of like how royalty passes down their leadership."

Sophie placed her elbows on the table and clasped her hands together. "And who would that be?"

"Nana, of course," Winnie replied.

"Of course," Sophie answered.

"No, she's not. Not anymore," Ted announced. His lips tilted up in the corners.

"If she's not, then who?" Marshall asked.

"Your wife," Ted answered while chewing his salad.

Marshall choked on his water, sputtering behind his hand before wiping the water away.

"You must be mistaken," Sophie said. "I'm the only one in my family with abilities. There is no way that I'm a descendent of the oldest family here."

Ted swallowed around his bite of salad. "You might want to check your family tree, sweetheart. I knew you looked familiar the day you moved in, so I started going through some of my old things. You might be surprised at what I found. I'm on kitchen detail tonight, but why don't you two stop by my place tomorrow? I'll let you take a look."

"We'd love to," Marshall announced. "Sophie baby, you don't look so hot."

"I'm fine." She tried to give Marshall a reassuring smile. "Just a long day."

Marshall rubbed her back. "Are you ready to go?"

She shook her head. "No, I'd like to meet some of the others before we call it a night."

Sophie and Marshall hung around and greeted those who approached the table and even afterward outside. Everyone was friendly enough. Most of them had already heard about the snake incident and about getting shot at in the woods. Word travelled fast among the coven members.

Marshall walked, with his arm around Sophie's shoulder, back to their cabin. Crickets chirped under the moonlight. Lights from surrounding houses illuminated the way back. Couples were settling in for a quiet night.

"I'm dying to know what the neighbor has on your family."

"I'm not," Sophie answered. "No one wants to be the last to find out family secrets. He must be mistaken."

Marshall pulled her closer, kissing the side of her head. "I hope for your sake you're right, or you might be here a lot longer than you thought."

Sophie smacked his midsection. "If I'm stuck, then you're stuck."

Marshall motioned to their surroundings. "I could live here."

Sophie tossed her head back and laughed the first real belly laugh since she'd arrived. "No, you couldn't. There isn't state-of-the-art anything, and you're not a hunter. You'd be bored stiff within the first week."

He dropped his hold and opened the door, letting her pass first. "But I'd have you, sugar butt."

"With words like those, I sure hope you're ready to show me your hammer."

He grinned and shut the door behind them, throwing the lock. He pulled her back against his chest, his lips right next to her ear. He whispered, "I'll take you right here, but I have to warn you, you'll be giving everyone a show. The only place we didn't set up surveillance is the bedroom and the bath."

She turned in his arms. "Is that what you've been doing all day?"

"That and more." He grinned and took her by the hand, leading her to the kitchen. He grabbed a pint of chocolate chip ice cream and handed it to her before grabbing the spoons.

"You do love me." Sophie grinned.

"I thought we'd already established that," Marshall answered.

"No....no, we haven't," she answered.

He took her spare hand and guided her to the bedroom. "Well then, let me rectify that."

Marshall closed the bedroom door behind him before meeting Sophie on the bed. She pulled the top off the ice cream and held her hand out for a spoon.

"Chocolate first and then the hammer." She grinned.

****

Marshall lay awake with Sophie in his arms, both depleted after hours of marathon sex. He lightly stroked her hair. He'd panicked when he saw the snake. The thought of losing her about crushed him. Could he protect her when even he was out of his element?

"Stop that."

"Stop what?" Marshall asked.

"I can hear you thinking,"

Marshall smiled. "I doubt that."

She drew circles on his chest. "I'm psychic, didn't you hear?"

His chest vibrated as he chuckled. "I might have heard something like that."

"Penny for your thoughts."

Marshall cleared his throat. "Sophie, I love you. I know I don't say it much."

"Much?" She leaned up on her arm to look him in the face. "This is your first."

"I love you." He ran his fingers through her hair, brushing the loose strands behind her ear.

She smiled. "This is a bad idea."

He rolled her, pressing her body into the bed. "Why? Why can't you just trust your feelings? Why can't you trust me and let me in?"

He watched her smile slip. Her gaze searched his, as though looking for an answer that he'd accept. "Marshall…"

Rolling off of her, he pushed off of the bed to stand. "It's okay, Sophie," he answered, giving her an easy out. He slid on his jeans and sat down, sliding on his shoes. "When you're ready, you'll tell me."

Sophie pulled the covers up over her chest, her eyes unsure. He couldn't convince her. He'd never be able to. It was a decision she'd have to come to on her own. "Where are you going?"

"Just going to do a perimeter check and make sure everything's quiet," he answered before leaning back over the bed. He pressed his lips to hers in a tender kiss. "I'll be back in a bit. Try and get some sleep."

She pressed her warm palm to his cheek and he leaned into her touch. "Marshall…"

"Shhh." He kissed her again. "I don't want you to say it just because I want to hear it. If you're unsure, then you're unsure. It will make it that much more special when you don't have any doubt."

Marshall walked out of the house, locking the door behind him. He pulled out his cell and dialed the office.

Beau yawned as he answered, "Hey, boss."

"I'm doing a perimeter check. Keep an eye on my girl."

"That might be possible if you'd put a camera in the bedroom."

"Not a chance." Marshall glanced up and down the deserted road. "No reason to show Aiden what he's missing."

"You've got company," Beau announced.

The statement caught him off guard.

"Is that what this is about?" Sophie asked from behind him. He turned to find her standing with the bed sheet wrapped around her body. "You're worried Aiden might make a move on me?"

"I've got to go," Marshall announced before hanging up and pocketing his phone.

He stepped closer to her. "I'm not worried he'll make a move, Sophie. I expect him to. He's a smart man." He cupped her cheek. "He knows a diamond when he sees one." He pulled her into his arms. His lips were mere inches from the creamy expanse of her neck. "If he was smart, he would have already tried."

She stepped out of his embrace. "Is this a game to you? Are you just with me to see if you could get me away from Jack? Do you guys have some bet on who can bed me?"

"No." Marshall closed the distance between them. He cupped her neck. "This is no game." He lifted her free hand and pressed it against his chest. "I love you."

And he meant every word he was saying. He watched as confusion clouded her face. Her face reddened from anger. He pressed his lips to hers in a crushing kiss, only easing when she leaned into his body and her heart raced like his. He rested his forehead against hers. "I've never lied to you. I've got some work to do. Go get some sleep."

He kissed her once more before stepping back. He had work to do, work that would keep her safe. That was what mattered right now. That was the only thing that mattered. He grabbed the backpack from the rear of the SUV and slung it over his arm before he started down the path in a jog.

7 CHAPTER

Sophie rolled in the bed and snuggled into the pillow she'd used in place of Marshall's body.

Her cell ringing had her prying her tired eyes opened. She rolled toward the alarm clock; the red numbers read four a.m. She grabbed her phone and answered it.

"Hello."

"Good morning, sunshine. I hear you miss me." Aiden crooned through the phone.

She wiped the sleep from her eyes. "Someone obviously lied to you. Why are you calling me at four a.m.?"

"We have a problem."

Sophie pulled the covers tighter around her chest and eased up into a sitting position. "What kind of a problem?"

"Where's Marshall?"

"I don't know," she answered. Pulling the covers around her body, she slid off the bed and walked through the house. "He isn't here. Did you try calling him?"

"We've been calling him for hours and no one is answering. Last night, we lost pictures on every single tree cam he placed in the woods. They aren't transmitting. So we have no eyes in the area, except for you."

Sophie paused in the hallway. "Were you originally getting pictures?"

There was a slight pause. "Yes. They worked for an hour and then all of them quit. One by one, they all went down."

Sophie hurried to the bedroom, dropping the sheet onto the floor. She grabbed clothes and threw them on the bed. "When was the last transmission?"

"Two hours ago, and Sophie….he was near the old cabins."

Sophie placed Aiden on speaker, dropped the phone onto the bed and started throwing on her clothes. "Why was he putting up the cams?"

Sophie tugged on her yoga pants and tee shirt, after twisting her hair up in a ponytail she shoved on socks and her boots. There was no way she was going into the woods with snakes and spiders without some type of protection on her feet.

"To see if he could catch the bastard that was shooting at you guys."

"Shit," Sophie cursed tying her lace with more force than was necessary.

"Well, the good news is he's still alive," Sophie announced, standing next to the bed. She grabbed one of Marshall's backpacks from the closet, picked up her phone, and headed back down the hall.

"How do you know that?"

"He'd be here haunting my ass if he weren't."

Sophie slid on her ring, enabling her GPS, before grabbing bottled waters out of the fridge and shoving them in the already full pack.

She rooted through the pack, checking the already packed items. A first aid kit, a change of clothes, a hunting knife and one of Marshall's guns rounded out the items. She grabbed her gun out of her purse and secured it in the leg strap that Marshall had given her a few months ago. "I'm going to look for him."

"Get a search team. Don't go alone."

"I don't trust any of them yet."

"Sophie, this isn't a good idea."

"Good thing I didn't ask for your opinion," she replied. "Keep the line open and start my ring tracer. I'll call you when I find him."

"Damn it, Sophie."

She heard him cussing as she hung up her phone and shoved it into her pocket.

She opened the sliding glass door and stepped out onto the dewy-morning grass.

She started in a jog toward the clump of trees directly behind the house. Her heart raced as the cool morning air chilled her cheeks. Half an hour into her search, the early morning temperature did little to cool her skin as she trampled through the thick green foliage. Her heart raced against her ribs. Her gaze darted around the woods, her fingers reaching for the gun handle at every sound she heard. She stayed quiet as she worked her way toward the old cabins. She passed one of the cameras on the ground and stopped. She squatted and picked up the broken black pieces. The strap was cut clean through. No animal had done this. This bastard was a human. The rattling sound of nearby snakes prompted her back to her feet and moving again.

Tears threatened to fall, and the farther she walked, the more her anxiety set in. What if something had happened to him? What if, God forbid, he was hurt or worse?

She stepped around trees through thick, uncut grass. A deer in the distance scurried off as she approached. A water stream trickled nearby. She continued deeper in, the large and thick trees shielding her from the sunrise.

Will appeared next to her in his ghostly presence.

"You have to hurry. You're almost out of time," he whispered before vanishing again.

She pushed through the bushes and came out into a clearing. She recognized the place immediately. She glanced to her left, and out in the distance, she saw what she was looking for. The place she'd almost died. "This can't be happening again."

She took off at a run, only slowing as she neared. She reached the side of the wooden shack and pressed her back against the wall. She pulled out her gun and held it close to her chest as she inched around to the front of the building. She stepped up onto the porch, the wood creaking beneath her feet.

Sophie moved to stand in front of the door, her gun positioned out in front of her in a tight grip, ready to shoot anything or one that might attack. She raised her boot and kicked. It took two times before it bowed inward and gave way.

Marshall was lying unconscious on the floor next to the cot where Sophie had been tied up when she'd been kidnapped before. A makeshift timer on a block of C4 was attached to the wall, and the red numbers of the timer were counting down. She stood motionless, not believing what she saw. Fear crept down her spine and into her bones. She swallowed around her dry throat, her heart thumping against her chest. They needed to get out and fast.

She hurried to his side. She placed her palms on his face. "Marshall, baby….you have to wake up."

She eyed the timer, less than five minutes to get him out. "A freakin' bomb." She glanced up at the ceiling. "Are you kidding me?"

"Marshall Dixon, I need you to wake your ass up," Sophie said while shaking Marshall's body. "We aren't going out like this. I just found you; I'm not ready to let you go."

Marshall's eyes fluttered open before closing again.

She moved behind him and grabbed beneath his arms, lifting his head off the ground. She used every muscle she didn't know she had trying to drag him out through the door she'd entered. Her gaze stayed steady on the timer, every tick ringing loudly in her ears.

She dug her feet in, thankful that she had the traction from her boots. She pulled, heaving as she did. A minute had ticked off and she'd barely made it into the other room. "Marshall, wake your ass up," she said through gritted teeth, pulling harder.

She'd just gotten him to the door when his eyes slid open. His brows dipped together. "What are you doing?"

"Saving your ass." She helped right him to his feet, grabbed him by the hand, and yelled, "Run."

They ran toward the tree line and had almost reached it when the bomb exploded behind them, knocking them to the ground. The loud explosion rocked through the woods. Wood and debris shot through the air and they both covered their heads. A sliver of wood sliced her arm. Her adrenaline masked any pain from the wood that was sticking out from her arm. She peeked beneath her arms after the rain of debris stopped.

She tossed her backpack off and rolled onto her back. Her chest heaved. She wiped the sweat from her brow and pulled the wood out of her arm, tossing it to the side. A fire roared from the remaining wood still attached to the foundation. The heat licked her skin as the black smoke climbed into the air.

"How did you find me?" Marshall asked, pushing up to sit. He felt the back of his head and his fingers came away bloody.

"The boys told me you went AWOL. Will told me I needed to hurry. He told me I was running out of time," she answered struggling for breath.

She turned her head to look at him. "What happened?"

Marshall shrugged. "I'm not sure. I set the cameras up around the woods and was about to set up the cottages, in the event the killer was using these to hide out, when I got hit from behind. That is all I remember."

She nodded and turned her gaze toward the rising sun, thankful she could see it for another day. "The cameras are toast."

Marshall clenched his eyes closed. "How many?"

"My guess is all of them. The guys don't have a signal and I found one on the ground. The strap was cut with a knife and the unit crushed."

"Shit."

Sophie pulled her phone out of her pocket and punched in Aiden's number. "I've got him. Send a fire truck and ambulance to the row of cabins in the back of the property."

"What the hell happened?" Aiden asked.

"A bomb exploded," she answered.

"Shit," Aiden replied.

"That's what Marshall said," Sophie replied. "I'm too tired to move. We'll be waiting on them."

She disconnected the call and tossed the phone down on the ground next to her.

He eased back down next to her and slid his fingers through hers. "You shouldn't have come alone."

"Next time don't work alone," she countered, "and I won't have to save you."

"Well, at least it wasn't for nothing," Marshall announced.

She turned her head, her mouth parted.

"Whoever left me in there knows explosives. That should help us narrow this son of a bitch down."

Ten minutes later, Sophie heard sirens wailing in the distance. She pushed herself up onto her elbows and watched as first a cop car pulled in followed by a fire truck and then an ambulance, all of them coming in through the back road around the property. A welcome sight for all involved. The EMT moved to her side, the bleeding cut evident and the only wound that could be seen.

Sophie used her head to gesture toward Marshall. "Him first. He was passed out when I found him. Mine is just a scratch."

The woman moved to stand behind Marshall and poked at his head. "We need to get some x-rays. Let's get you on a stretcher."

"I'm not going anywhere without her."

Sophie let out a deep breath and pushed herself to her feet. "You aren't using me as an excuse. Let's go, you big baby."

Another EMT had Sophie's arm bent in an unnatural angle, trying to get a better look at her cut through the blood running from her arm.

"Scratch, huh?" He smirked.

Bastard.

****

Sophie glanced at the ring on her finger as she sat in Marshall's hospital room waiting for them to wheel him back in. Marshall needed a tracker. He was the one taking the risks. She had almost lost him today. Hell, she'd almost gotten herself killed in the process.

"Don't get too fond of that," Jack announced as he entered the room.

Sophie held her hand up higher and moved it around, watching the overhead light shine off the stones. "Why? I think it's growing on me."

"Marshall should have been wearing that last night," Aiden said, sidestepping around Jack. "Then we could have found him and let you sleep in."

Sophie smiled. "That would have been nice. The idea of my bed sounds fantastic."

Aiden leaned down and hugged her and kissed her hair. "I suggest you shower first. You smell like smoke."

She shrugged. "A fire tends to do that to a girl."

"Sophie…" Jack started to say.

"It's too late, Jack. You can't get me fired." She grinned. "I'm a partner."

Jack's mouth dropped open as he cursed beneath his breath.

"Where's Marshall?"

"Getting x-rays. He took a blow to the back of the head."

Jack's eyes opened wide.

"And you saved his ass again." Aiden held up his fist for a bump.

She grinned and bumped it. "I've learned from the best. Although, you might want to add explosive training to your curriculum. If he hadn't come to while I was dragging him out, we wouldn't have made it in time."

Jack turned around and stalked out without even looking back.

"If I didn't know any better, you might be a guardian angel."

"I think that should be her new nickname," Marshall announced as they wheeled him into the room.

"It's better than sugar butt."

Aiden grinned. "Sugar butt?" He glanced at her. "You didn't kick his ass for that one?"

"I couldn't. There were too many witnesses. You haven't taught me how to be covert."

"That's the next lesson, after explosive training."

Marshall shook his head and grinned before being helped onto the bed.

"You're here overnight," the nurse announced. "You might as well get comfortable." She dropped his chart in the box on the door on her way out.

"Concussed?" Aiden asked. "Do I need to keep Sophie company while you get poked and prodded all night?"

Sophie rolled her eyes. "I need a shirt that reads, *Have gun. Will shoot.*"

"Actually, I was thinking that wouldn't be a bad idea." Marshall leaned back against the pillow, letting out a long breath. "She shouldn't be alone. Not with this asshole's training."

"And exactly how do you expect me to explain that to the coven members? My husband is laid up in the hospital and I have another man coming over to stay with me?" She shook her head. "They'll have me labeled a charlatan and probably string me up by my toes."

"Nah, they're like hippies. They probably have orgies and crap. Maybe I should come and hang out." Aiden grinned like a teenage about to have all of his fantasies come true.

"You aren't coming home with me," Sophie said before turning to Marshall. "And you should stay the night and through the afternoon tomorrow. That way we have a valid excuse not to attend the ceremony."

"What am I missing?" Aiden asked.

"Nothing," they both clipped out.

"I'm out of here as soon as I see a doctor, Mrs. Dixon. You can count on it."

Sophie rose from her chair and planted her fists on her hips. "Yeah? And how exactly do you plan to protect me when you can't shoot straight and you're sleeping?"

The room remained silent.

She walked over to the bed and pressed a kiss to his lips. "I'll work it out," she answered against his lips. "Don't worry about me." She righted her stance and winked. "Just get some sleep." She tilted her head. "I think that was the last thing you said to me. I've got to go make up some lame-ass excuse why a building blew up on their property and we were involved. I'll check in on you later."

She patted Aiden's chest in passing. "Why don't you play babysitter and make sure my husband stays put? That will help me." She grinned and walked out the door.

Sophie made it out of the hospital without anyone talking to her or trying to kill her. Someone at the coven had tried to kill her husband. Someone was out to kill them both. She took a deep, calming breath as she ran though different revenge scenarios in her head. She dialed Amber's number.

"Can you come get me?"

"Sure, hon. Where are you?"

"At the hospital."

****

Sophie slid into the passenger seat of Amber's car and pulled the door closed.

"How's the case?" She glanced at the bandage on Sophie's arm. "And what happened to your arm?"

"It's a long story, but flying wood happened to my arm, and we're no closer to solving the case than when we started. Maybe if I could figure out what the motive is, then the pieces would fall into place."

"Maybe you need a fresh prospective. What do you have so far?"

Amber was the best friend anyone could have. It was in her blood to help.

"We know that those killed were from covens; their partners didn't have gifts; and now we know the perp is trained with guns and explosives. That's all we know." She shrugged. "If you don't count that one of my relatives possibly had abilities and it was kept from us when we were growing up."

Amber's mouth briefly parted before she snapped it closed. She turned down the long road headed toward the outskirts of town. "Okay, well when I think motive, I think money, power and revenge. I'm sure there are more, but those three come to mind. Do any of those fit with the people you've met?"

Sophie leaned her head back in the seat and let her mind replay everything that had happened and everyone she'd met since arriving. "Money, no... The coven doesn't need any, well, not that I can tell."

Sophie made a mental note to check with Piper when she got back.

"What about revenge?"

Sophie couldn't think of anyone hating Mary. She wasn't that type of woman. "I can't think of anything or anyone who would have wanted her harmed."

"Maybe they were looking for power...Mary was the leader, and now she'll be replaced via vote."

"Maybe someone will have a lot to gain from her death," Amber suggested

Sophie's eyes widened and she turned in her seat. "You're brilliant."

"I don't know what I said." Amber grinned. "But thanks, you're not too shabby yourself."

Sophie pulled out her phone and fired off a text to Beau, asking him to check the status of the deceased members at the other covens and what implications their deaths had on whoever took over. Maybe there was a link or a common thread. Maybe this asshole was a hit for hire or the person responsible gained something from the deaths.

Amber turned into the coven. "Where am I dropping you off?"

Sophie pointed to the common area building. "I need to talk to Piper and then I'll walk back to our house."

Amber pulled up and put the car into park. "I hear you and Marshall are getting pretty serious. You're sister-in-law filled me in on your cover, but still…"

Sophie had her hand on the door handle and glanced back at her friend. "We're dating, but that's it."

Amber's gaze landed on the ring on Sophie's finger. "Have you decided you want more?"

Sophie opened the door and got out, sticking her head back in the car. "You know….I thought I lost him this morning, and that freaked me out."

Amber gave a slow nod. "It would have freaked anyone out."

Sophie shook her head. "It was more than that. I couldn't breathe thinking of a life without him, and I wasn't going to leave him there to die. It would have killed me either way. With him or without him."

Amber gave a sad smile. "Then I guess you have your answer."

"I don't know," Sophie answered. "I love him." Sophie took a long deep breath. "Do you think it's too soon? Jack and I…."

Amber finished the sentence. "Are over. Don't compare them. Those two are like night and day."

Sophie dropped her gaze to the seat before lifting it to look Amber in the eyes. "And thick as thieves."

She stood and closed the door, waving as she watched Amber head back out of the coven. This was her life, her screwed-up, fucked-up life. She was damned even if she did love Marshall. Jack would never be okay with the union, not if it was real.

8 CHAPTER

Sophie jogged up onto the porch and walked through the common area. She headed straight for Piper's office and knocked lightly on the door. No one answered.

She knocked again before turning the knob and peeking inside.

"She's not here," Winnie said from the hallway. "She heard about the building blowing up and no one has seen her since. The police came by wanting to ask her questions and they couldn't find her either."

Sophie pulled the door closed. "Has anyone looked in her apartment?"

Winnie shrugged. "I think so." She pointed toward the stairs. "It's the top floor, last one on the left. Maybe she came back."

Sophie smiled around her fear that maybe something had also happened to the coven's leader. "Thanks, I think I'll go check."

Taking the stairs two at a time, Sophie climbed up the three flights and headed down the hall. She'd never been in the upstairs area. Everything was white and light and airy. Windows at the end of the hall let in a good amount of light, reflecting off the white walls. Flowers were strategically placed on tables at the end. The doors looked like bedroom doors with standard-issue locks that needed a key. Locks that could be picked, if the need arose.

Sophie stopped in front of the last door on the left and knocked. No one answered. Maybe the woman was off meditating somewhere, or hell, maybe she'd gone to visit another coven. There were plenty of explanations on where she might be.

"I think I'll just take a peek," she whispered in the empty hallway before pulling a credit card out of her purse. She shoved it between the jam and the lock, thankful that it popped open and there wasn't a deadbolt or chain on the door. She slipped inside, easing the door shut behind her.

She turned to find Piper's room in shambles. Furniture was overturned, the cushions sliced through and stuffing pulled out. What had once been a ceramic lamp was shattered on the floor. Books were pushed off the shelf, several open and on the floor.

"Piper," Sophie called out as she stepped farther into the room, careful not to touch anything. "Are you in here?"

No one answered. Sophie balled her fists to keep from automatically grabbing the stuff and righting them. Her brother would kill her for contaminating any remaining evidence. She eased down the hall. Her heart raced in her chest. The hair on the nape of her neck stood on end. All three doors were ajar. None of the other rooms were as messy as the living room. Using her foot, she nudged the bedroom door the rest of the way open. The bedroom was clean. The bed was made. The room looked untouched, as if the perp didn't have time to check the rest of the place or maybe hadn't needed too.

As Sophie turned to leave the room, her gaze landed on Piper's dresser. A familiar pendant sat on top, a piece of jewelry Sophie had seen before, one that Mary had shown her and had always worn. Sophie walked into the bathroom, took some tissue and used it to pick up the piece. Fear and anger coursed through her veins. She swallowed around the lump in her throat, almost afraid to turn the piece over. The one Sophie had seen had Mary's name on the back. The piece had been a gift from the coven when she'd assumed the role as leader, a protection piece that she never left home without wearing. Sophie flipped it over and her heart sank into her stomach. Mary's name was etched on the back.

Only the killer would have had the opportunity to take the jewelry. Only the killer would have kept the souvenir, just as they had kept the other missing pieces.

"Well, I didn't see that coming," Sophie announced, unsure what to do with the item. She walked through the apartment and into the kitchen. She needed to leave this somewhere safe, without her fingerprints preferably, while she went looking for Piper. She had to find the woman. Sophie needed answers.

She wrapped the piece in the tissue and lifted a flowerpot sitting on the windowsill in the kitchen. She stuck it underneath, leaving it behind. She grabbed a paper towel and stepped over the broken furniture and glass on the way to the door. She used the towel to wipe off her prints and turn the knob, using it on the outer knob to close the door behind her.

Sophie jogged down the stairs until she reached the emergency exit. She pushed through the door, thankful she was back outside. She glanced over her shoulder and quickened her pace. There were people milling around outside, some in the pavilion and others on the path. People were watching her. She forced herself to slow down and pulled her phone from her pocket. Her find was too important not to tell someone else in the event of her kidnapping or demise. Someone else needed to know. Her hands shook as she fired off a text to Aiden, praying he was still at the hospital with Marshall. She told him what she'd found and where she'd hidden it and asked that he give Marshall the information.

Her phone rang seconds after hitting Send.

"Hello."

"Where the hell are you?" Marshall demanded.

"Oh hi, honey," Sophie answered casually as a couple passed her. "I'm on the road to our place."

"You can't talk?"

"No….not really. So how are you feeling?"

"Was she there?"

"No, I'm fine," she continued in code until she was farther away from anyone who might overhear.

"She wasn't there and her apartment was trashed," Sophie whispered into the phone. "Winnie told me no one has seen her since the explosion."

"Are you sure it was Mary's?"

"Yep."

"So someone either planted it there or she's the killer."

"I don't know," Sophie answered through gritted teeth. "My weapon is in the backpack." Sophie glanced around nervously.

"I have them stashed around the house. There's one in the knife drawer in the kitchen. It's similar to yours and loaded. Use that one. I'm on my way."

"Marshall, you can't leave."

"Like hell. I'll be there in twenty minutes, and Sophie….watch your back until I get there."

"But…" The line went dead before she could argue. He was coming home regardless of whether she wanted him to or not.

She let out a long breath.

"Hey," a male said from behind her.

Sophie spun around, her hand clenching the phone against her chest. Nana's nephew, Kevin, stood behind her. He'd appeared out of nowhere.

"You scared me."

"Sorry." He nodded toward her arm. "I heard you and your husband were almost killed. From the looks of it, you were just a little banged up." Kevin glanced around the area. "Where's your husband?"

Sophie took a tentative step back. "He's on his way. He should be back any minute."

"Well then, I need to make this quick," he announced and reached for something beneath his jacket.

Sophie didn't stop to think. She grabbed his arm, turned her body, and flipped him over her shoulder until he was lying sprawled out on the ground.

"Aw....what the hell did you do that for?" he asked. His brows were dipped in confusion as he looked up at her.

Sophie moved the jacket aside. Sticking out of his waistband wasn't a gun, but a book?

"I...I'm so sorry." She held out her hand to help him up. "I'm just real edgy from the explosion this morning. I thought...." She shook her head. "Never mind what I thought. I'm sorry."

He rose and brushed the dirt from his pants. He pulled the book out and held it out to her. "I just thought you might like a copy of the coven's rules and by-laws. You'll need them if you decide to stay." Kevin boyishly kicked the dirt around with his foot. "I hope you do. I'd love to learn about your gifts."

She took the book and held it against her chest. "Thanks, I'm not sure what we're going to do yet. I'm not sure I'll be able to talk Marshall into staying after the house incident. I heard the cops are saying it was a gas leak."

Kevin's brows dipped. "I hadn't heard that yet, but it's good to know." He gestured with his thumb over his shoulder. "I've got dinner duty and have to go." He pointed to the book. "Let me know if you have any questions."

Before she could even answer, he'd turned and started jogging down the street.

"Strange one, that boy." Sophie spun around again and came face to face with her neighbor.

"You guys have got to stop sneaking up on me, or you'll give me a heart attack," she announced, her chest heaving again.

"Sorry, I heard about the shack and saw you out here with Kevin. I figured you might need saving."

Sophie started walking toward her house. Ted kept in step with her.

"Have you seen Piper?" Sophie asked. "I really need to talk to her."

"Nope, can't say that I have. Did you try the common area or her apartment?"

"Yeah," Sophie answered. "I did."

She took a long deep breath, a headache forming behind her eyes. "I'm not feeling so hot. I think I'm going to go lie down until Marshall gets back."

He gave her a worried smile. "I'll be right next door if you need me. Don't forget, I have that information to show you."

"I won't, and thanks for everything."

She stepped up onto her porch, pulled the key from her pocket, and turned the knob. Her heart almost leapt from her chest for the third time in fifteen minutes. Roman was sitting in the recliner and Dash on her couch. Dash was looking down at his phone, probably surfing the Internet.

She hurried and shut the door. "What are you two doing here?"

"Well, we were told you didn't want to be alone with Aiden for fear of your reputation, so we decided to take his place." Dash grinned. "You could have warned us you didn't have a TV."

"You could have warned me you were coming." She peeked out of the blinds. "Did anyone see you?"

"What do you think we are...amateurs? You must have us confused with your ex."

Sophie let the blinds fall back into place. "I'm kind of glad you're here." She headed to the kitchen and pulled out the Glock from the knife drawer and a beer from the fridge. "My nerves are shot and I need a bath."

"Do you need help?" Dash asked.

"Nope, but you're sounding more and more like Aiden every day."

Dash held his hand up to his heart. "That hurt, Sophie."

"I'm learning from the best." She grinned and headed down the hall. A warm bath was calling her name. Some flowery shampoo to kill the smell of smoke in her hair and some relaxing bath salt to ease her aches. She signed in contentment just thinking about it.

***

Marshall opened the bathroom door and poked his head in. "Don't shoot."

Sophie chuckled. "I wouldn't dream of it."

He walked in and shut the door behind him. "Are you enjoying your bubble bath?"

Sophie relaxed against the back of the tub. Her wet strands were dripping down her bare chest, the rest of her body hidden beneath lucky bubbles.

"Yes. It's divine."

Marshall kicked off his boots and ditched his socks. He reached behind him and tugged the shirt off his back, letting it fall onto the floor. He unbuckled his jeans and pulled those and his boxers down and stood in front of her naked. He reached for his cock and gave one long tug before making her scoot up. He climbed in behind her, engulfing her in his arms.

She leaned back against his chest and a purr left her lips. "Did you have to sneak out?"

Marshall chuckled. "I don't sneak, baby. I just walked out."

Sophie looked up at him. "I'm glad you're okay."

He kissed her forehead. "I'm glad you saved me."

She grinned before turning to face front again. She splashed some of the bubbles up onto her chest and lifted her hand out of the water, watching as the water rolled off. Her fingers were pruned, but it didn't look as if she was getting out any time soon.

His cock pressed against her backside, unable to hide the need he felt for her. "You know...they say it's natural after a near-death experience to want to feel alive again."

Her chest rumbled as she laughed. "Don't tell me...you want to go zip lining or bungee jumping?"

She rose onto her knees and turned in the water. She maneuvered so she straddled his lap. "Or do you want to feel me?"

She slid down on his shaft and he couldn't control his moan of pleasure. Her tight sheath wrapped around him, sucking him in as she lifted and slid back down.

He held her waist, easing her up and down, letting her feel every inch of him. "Damn, Sophie. You feel so good."

"I can make you feel better." She leaned forward and pressed her lips to his before she moved faster, splashing water outside of the tub.

He needed her, and she gave herself willingly. He lifted his hips to match her need.

Fifteen minutes later, she collapsed against his chest. Her lips lingered against his in a kiss before she moved and retook her spot. She told him about everything that had happened since leaving the hospital. Piper's room, her find, and then getting stopped in the street. He'd been rubbing her arms, careful of her wet bandage. She mentioned Kevin and his movements stilled.

"Well, sounds like we need to get ready for dinner. It's time we go figure out what all of the gossip is on Piper and see what we can find out."

Sophie stood and grabbed her towel, wrapping it around her body. She stepped out. "I think you're right. I'll start getting dressed while you finish up in here."

She leaned over and pressed her lips to his once more before disappearing out of the bathroom.

Marshall watched her leave. Would their relationship ever be normal? Could he give her the life she deserved, one that didn't include their lives on the line? Guns stashed around the house? Was he being selfish by wanting her in his life? She'd almost died because of his mistakes. If the blast hadn't killed him, her dying would have. His heart clenched tight. Was Jack right when he didn't think she could handle the danger?

9 CHAPTER

"Okay, next time warn us," Roman announced as Sophie walked out of the bedroom. "Or at least supply the ear plugs." He shook his head. "Princess, you get loud when you're getting your freak on."

Sophie laughed, not caring if her face reddened. "You're just jealous you weren't responsible for those moans."

Dash grinned. "Yep, and now I understand why they put you in the last house on this row. They were afraid you'd keep everyone awake. So have you gotten freaky outside yet? In the pavilion or against a tree or were you worried that cameras would catch you in the act and your sex tape would make it on the Internet?"

"Cameras!" Sophie exclaimed. "I'm such an idiot. Is Beau at work?"

"Damn well better be," Roman answered.

She pulled out her phone and dialed the number. "I need the video surveillance of the common area, from the bottom floor to the top. Can you access it?"

"Piece of cake," Beau answered. "What am I looking for?"

"Piper and anyone who entered her residence on the top floor. Last door on the left. I want to know everyone coming and going. Even if you don't have their names, send me their faces."

"Copy that," Beau answered. "Hey, Soph…."

"Yeah."

"Aiden wants to talk to you."

Sophie tried to hide her surprise and moved into the kitchen.

"You don't honestly think the guys didn't notice you finding a quieter place to talk, did you?" Aiden asked.

She turned to find both of them looking at her.

"I forgot you can see us." She grinned. "Did you need something?"

She moved to the fridge and grabbed a bottle of water.

"There are fifteen men and three women at your compound with past military experience, not including our guys. You need to be careful."

She turned to lean against the breakfast counter. "So all of them know how to move through the woods?"

"Yep."

"Crap," she replied. "Any on that list have prior medical experience?"

There was a pause on the line. "I didn't notice. Why do you ask?"

"Mary wasn't a small woman, and she wouldn't have been coerced easily. In the picture Marshall had, there was a small puncture mark on her neck. Did they run a toxicology report on her? Did she have anything in her system?"

"Shit. I didn't even notice." Aiden's voice filled the line with a string of curses. "Let me see what I can find. I'll call you back."

Sophie's voice dropped to a whisper. "Thanks, A."

"Be careful, Soph. Someone has already tried to kill you twice. I'd hate to have to go commando on the coven if you wind up dead."

Sophie chuckled. "You'd do that for me?"

"Do what?" Marshall asked, as he stepped out of the hallway.

"If I died, Aiden would go all commando," she replied.

Marshall slid the phone out of Sophie's hand. "Quit hitting on my wife."

He hung up the phone, kissed her forehead and headed back into the living room.

"Wait....that was what you guys call flirting?" Sophie asked, following behind Marshall into the living room. She plopped down on the arm of the chair where Marshall was sitting. He rubbed a circle on the small of her back.

"Sophie, he offered violence. Of course he was flirting."

"Have you guys considered buying chocolates, flowers, or hell, even shoes? At least the women would know what the hell you were doing. You guys need some serious help." Her stomach grumbled. "And we need to get going if we're going to be early enough to eat the good food."

"Hey….what about us?" Dash asked.

"Frozen pizza in the freezer and beer in the fridge. I need you guys here tonight. I hope you didn't have plans."

"Nope," Roman announced, kicking his feet up on the coffee table. "Nowhere to be."

Marshall slid his fingers through hers and led the way out of the house and started walking down the path. Every muscle in his body was rigid, not like a guy that had just gotten laid. Even his jaw ticked.

"Why were you talking to Aiden?" He paused as if choosing the words he wanted to use. "Were you leading him on?"

"Excuse me!" she asked, pulling him to a stop. "Did I just hear you right?"

Marshall shrugged. "Well, if the shoe fits."

"Oh no." Sophie crossed her arms over her chest and shook her head. "You are not doing this. You are not going to push me away because of the freakin bomb."

"This has nothing to do with that." Marshall said. "We're talking about Aiden."

His hateful accusations didn't match the love she could still read in his eyes. "No, we're not. What are you afraid of Marshall? You went from husband to asshole in two seconds flat. What is going on?"

"Honey, you haven't begun to see asshole. What did you expect when I hear my fucking wife on the phone flirting." Marshall raised his voice. "Tell me, Sophie. Were you lining things up to have him waiting in the wings?"

Sophie stalked closer to Marshall. She slapped him with her open hand across the face. Her palm stung. "Screw you, Marshall."

"You already did, sugar."

"We're done, Marshall. If you can't even be honest with me, then at least be honest with yourself."

"Honest....you want honesty? What am I supposed to think when you jump from Jack to his best friend? It makes perfect sense that you might be lining up Aiden to have him next."

Her mouth parted, a bit dazed and stunned that the asshole had the nerve to go there of all places. Was he on crack? "Jack and I were over before I ever let you in....you schmuck."

Sophie spun around on her heels and jogged back toward the house. She fought the tears clouding her eyes. She walked into the house and slammed the door behind her. The men in the kitchen turned to look at her and she stomped by them to the bedroom, slamming that door as she did.

"I can't believe I fell for his shit." She seethed and paced the length of the room and back, over and over. "If he thinks…" Grrrr. She growled, picked up her brush from the bed, and threw it at the wall above the bed, knocking a picture off the wall. The fall was cushioned by her mattress. Where was a punching bag when she needed one?

"Sophie," Roman said from the other side of the door. "You need to come out here."

"Go away," She replied.

"You've got a visitor," Roman announced.

Sophie paused in her tracks at those words. Who the heck would be stopping by her house when everyone else should be eating supper?

She pulled the door open and walked out into the living room. Winnie stood between Roman and Dash. Her face was white, all of the blood drained away.

"I...I...I'm sorry to interrupt," she started before pausing to look up at the men she was standing between.

"Don't mind them. They're just my cousins, in town for a visit."

Winnie gave a slow nod. She held out a note. "I was in Piper's office, looking for the keys to the wine cellar, and I found this in her drawer."

Sophie walked over to the woman. The envelope was sealed and it had Sophie's name written on the front.

Sophie turned and slid her finger beneath the flap. She pulled out the letter and opened it.

Sophie,

I had a vision that my letter would find you. I've been targeted. I've seen my death and I had to leave. The afternoon of the explosion, I was going to die. I'm praying that my destiny has changed since my dream. I pray that I got out before I was next. I don't know the reason or who the man is. He was wearing a ski mask. I just know that he was coming. I'm sorry for dragging you into this mess. It's not too late for you to leave too. My vision switched from my death to yours. Your body was found in the woods. Whatever you do, stay out of them. Whoever is doing these killings knows them well. Too well.

Be safe, my friend, and don't trust anyone. No one. For I fear that the killer's blood runs strong in the foundation of the coven.

Piper

Sophie spun around to find all gazes set on hers.

"Well?" Winnie asked. "Does it say where she went?"

Sophie folded the letter and stuffed it back into the envelope. "She had a family emergency. She didn't have time to explain, just that she needed to leave."

"I wonder why she didn't tell anyone," Winnie said, about to take a tentative step in Sophie's direction. She then probably thought better of it when Roman cleared his throat.

"I don't know. I guess we'll have to ask her when she returns."

Winnie's brows rose. "Did she mention when that might be?"

"I'm afraid not." Sophie shook her head while folding the envelope in half and stuffing it into her back pocket. She walked over to the door and held it open. "Thank you for bringing this to me."

"Oh." Winnie walked to the door and out onto the porch. "You're welcome. I'm just glad she's all right."

"Me too," Sophie replied.

Winnie gestured over her shoulder. "Did you guys want to come eat? I thought I passed your husband on the way here."

Sophie pasted a fake smile on her lips. "Oh no, thank you. I wanted to spend some time with my cousins."

"Okay," Winnie answered before spinning on her heels and walking off. Sophie shut the door and peeked through the blinds before turning back to Dash and Roman.

"What was all that about, *cousin*?"

"Appears Piper feared for her life and ran."

Sophie walked into the kitchen and grabbed a beer.

"And?" Dash prodded.

"And what?" she answered, popping the top off and tossing it in the garbage.

"Where's Marshall?" Dash asked.

"I'm not sure I care right now," she replied. "As a matter of fact, I think I'll call one of my other million boyfriends. One that isn't afraid I'm going to get myself killed. He's just like Jack. I should have known."

Dash and Roman exchanged a look. "He accused you of cheating on him?" Roman asked.

"But you two just..." Dash cut himself off before finishing his statement.

"I'd rather not talk about it." She took a long swig of her beer. "I'm going for a hike in the woods."

"At night?" Roman asked.

"Yep," she replied. "The quicker I solve this case, the sooner I can move on with my life."

"Wait…you can't leave us. You're a partner," Dash said, moving to stand next to her. "Whatever he did can be fixed."

She shook her head, refusing to shed any tears. "This is a ruse, Dash. He doesn't love me, and if I had to guess, I don't think he ever did. I was a game to be won. Nothing more, nothing less. He just didn't want his best friend to win."

"You're joking, right?" Roman asked.

"I wish I were." She walked into the bedroom and grabbed the gun from the dresser drawer. She picked up one of the spare backpacks and walked back out into the room.

Dash took the backpack out of her hands and Roman took the gun. "Sit down and tell us what happened."

She folded her arms across her chest, fighting back the tears. She told them everything. She didn't know why she did it, or how she managed while fighting the tears, but she spilled her guts to the two men who knew her least.

Dash had a menacing look on his face. Roman had a grin on his. Their reactions were opposite.

"I'll kill him." Dash balled his fists by his sides.

Roman smirked. "You couldn't even if you tried." He shook his head. "We're going to do worse. By the time we're done, he'll wish he was dead."

Roman pulled the phone out of his pocket and fired off a series of texts. He turned back to them. "Sophie, you'll sleep on the couch tonight. We'll take the floor."

"We will?" Dash asked.

"Yep. Reinforcements will be here in the morning. Marshall is officially off the case."

"Wait, how can you do that?" Sophie asked.

"I'm calling a family meeting. He may have the majority vote, but seeing as Sophie's his wife, she owns half of everything he owns."

"That's only in a divorce, dumbass," Dash replied.

"And assuming we're really married," Sophie exclaimed. "Besides, I don't want his company. I don't want anything from him. Not even his vote. I just want…."

"What?" Roman asked. "What is it you want, Sophie?"

"I want the ache to go away. I'm tired of every man in my life thinking I'm screwing them over and not believing in me. I don't want to do this anymore. None of it. I want to find the killer and throw him in jail so he won't hurt anyone, and then I want out."

Roman plopped down on the sofa and patted the seat next to him. She moved to sit beside him. "Then that's what you'll get. We'll find this asshole and then we'll get you out. You have my word."

Sophie's chest heaved and she leaned against Roman's shoulder. "I wish it were that easy."

"It is," Dash explained.

"I have to marry him tomorrow," she said, her voice soft. "It's a ritual that the coven performs. They'll expect us."

"Then you'll marry him." Roman tossed his arm around her shoulders. "And once this is over, I'm sure we can find an attorney to perform an annulment. I'm sure his ex would be happy to do it for free."

Sophie's phone buzzed and she read the text. Her frown eased into a semi smile as she rose. "I have to go meet Aiden at the office. He's got my list ready."

"Can't he just email it to you?"

"No, he has a whole file on a few of the members. I need to go to the office." She grabbed the keys from the counter and walked to the door.

"What do you want us to tell Marshall when he gets back?"

"I don't care what you tell him," She answered as she walked out the door. "I'll be back in a bit. You two play nice."

They grinned. Dash laced his fingers behind his head. "Oh, we'll play nice. Don't you worry about a thing."

10 CHAPTER

Marshall stood just inside the door of the common room, his gaze scanning the area. "I'm such a dumbass. She's right and she deserves better."

"You sound like a wise man," Nana announced from behind him and wrapped her palm around his arm. They were flanked by her nephews. "I'm surprised really."

Marshall led the old woman across the noisy room. "Why is that?"

"You haven't been married long enough to come to that realization. You must have screwed up pretty bad if she didn't even want to eat dinner with you."

Marshall pulled out the old woman's chair and waited for her to sit. "You can say that again."

Nana waited for Marshall to sit before crossing her arms on the table and leaning forward. "If you already know this, then what are you doing here?"

"Letting her cool off." Marshall leaned back in his chair. "I said some pretty nasty things."

"Did you mean them?"

He shook his head. "No."

"Sounds like you've got your work cut out for you." She pointed a long, bony finger at Marshall. "Depends on what length you'll go to, to fix things."

"It's better this way." Marshall leaned back in his chair. "Better." He resigned.

"Then you're not as smart as I thought. I know love when I see it, sonny…and that girl loves you."

"I can't give her what she wants. I was a fool to think I could. I got scared and pushed her away."

"Then apologize and tell her you were wrong. It's that simple and yet that hard."

Marshall folded his arms on the table in front of him. "Are you women always right?"

She grinned and folded her hands in her lap. "Let me give you a piece of advice." The lines around her mouth deepened as she pressed her lips together. "The way to make a woman happy is through her heart. It's in your nature to want to fix things, but you can't use your muscles to fix everything. You have to start with fixing the heart before you can fix the rest. She can't read your mind. You're going to have to let her in if you want to keep her. It will go a long way toward fixing whatever you did wrong." She grinned. "Because you were wrong, that's lesson number two."

Kevin returned with a plate and drink, setting it down in front of her. Kevin sat down next to her with Franklin on the other side. Franklin slid a plate in front of Marshall. The move was unexpected.

"There are only two questions you have to ask yourself."

One of the others came by the table, interrupting whatever Nana was going to say. She poured Marshall and Franklin a glass a tea before disappearing.

"Do you love her and does she love you? If the answers are yes, then you two will work it out."

Marshall took a sip of his tea and contemplated those questions. He did love Sophie, but the question remained if she loved him. He believed in her. He trusted her and he loved her. What the hell had he done? He should have just been honest with her instead of trying to run her off by being mean. He'd almost lost her today and that thought scared the shit out of him so he'd done the only thing he could think of. He'd pushed her away and used Aiden as an excuse. Marshall was a bigger idiot than Jack when it came to Sophie. He should have just told her the truth and let the pieces fall where they may.

Nana was watching him like a hawk. Her head was tilted to the side and she stared at him, as if trying to read his mind. She leaned forward. "You're a smart man, Marshall Dixon. What are you still doing here?"

Marshall rose from his chair and walked by the old woman, squeezing her shoulder as he passed. He didn't honestly think Sophie was screwing around on him. He'd said those things to push her away. To make her see that they weren't right together. He'd done exactly what Jack had done. He stepped off the common area porch. He needed to go home; he needed his wife; he needed what mattered most. "Shit."

"Mr. Dixon." Winnie stopped him in front of the common area. "Are Sophie's cousins staying long?"

"Cousins?"

"Yeah, the guys at your house. Will they be here long?"

The woman was clearly talking about Roman and Dash. "You stopped by my house?"

"Yeah." She looked down at her feet before meeting his gaze. "I had to give her a letter from Piper. Are those men here for the vow renewal?"

Marshall's lips twitched. He'd forgotten all about the vow renewal. Something Sophie would probably fight with her last breath. "Yes, yes they are. Sophie wanted her family around to witness it this time." Marshall lowered his voice. "They still don't believe our marriage is official since we sealed the deal in Vegas."

Winnie smiled. "Okay. Have a good night."

She left him standing outside the common area and he watched her walk into the building. He started back to his house. His pace slowed. What was he going to tell her? How was he going to apologize? How was he going to fix this with an audience? He knew his partners better than anyone. If they knew what he'd done, they wouldn't let him within three feet of her much less leave her vulnerable so he could talk to her.

He walked up to his house. The lights were on inside, but the SUV was gone. Had Dash and Roman left? Hope bloomed in his chest that maybe he could have some alone-time with her to explain what was going on in his head. Why he'd freaked out.

He walked in to find Dash and Roman in the living room. Each had a half-eaten pizza on their plates and a few empty beer bottles were sitting around.

"Where's the SUV?" he asked.

"Isn't the better question, where's your wife?" Roman asked.

Marshall crossed his arms over his chest. "Okay…where's my fucking wife?"

Dash shared a look with Roman before answering. He shrugged. "Maybe she's out enjoying her bachelorette party."

"No…I think she mentioned going out to fuck all of her ex-boyfriends and the ones she has waiting in the wings for when she dumps your sorry ass."

Marshall's head dropped forward and he shook his head. "She told you?"

"Dude, I'm not complaining. I plan on making my move next if I can beat Aiden to the punch," Dash announced while standing up. "And don't think for a minute that I'd let her go. I know who she is, what she is, and what she brings to the table. I'm not afraid to be with her, unlike you."

Marshall met Dash's gaze head-on. The need to pummel him was riding heavy in his chest. "She almost died today."

Roman picked up his beer and took a sip. "The bomb didn't kill her, Marshall. You did that all by yourself." He set his beer down. "For someone who's loved her from the beginning, what the hell were you thinking?"

Marshall folded his arms over his chest. "What was I thinking?" His shoulders sagged as the anger left his body. He plopped down in the chair and rested his elbows on his knees. "I was thinking that she almost died saving my life." He met their gazes. "I can't lose her."

"You already did," Dash announced. "She's with Aiden."

"Not for long," Marshall announced. His heart reawakened; the haze in his brain dissipated. He wanted her; he needed her, and it was high time she realized what the hell that meant.

"Where's your car?" He ground his teeth together.

"We left it outside the gate and scaled the wall, coming in on foot." Roman tossed Marshall the keys. "She's ready to walk. Go fix it."

"I plan on it," Marshall announced.

****

Aiden answered his cell at the same time he spotted Sophie on the security cameras walking into the building. He'd just witnessed Marshall on the cameras. He'd heard every word exchanged both when Sophie explained what happened and now with Marshall. The shithead was on his way and Sophie didn't have a clue.

Aiden's desire for her warred with doing the right thing. Could Marshall make her happy, keep her happy? Did he even know how? Her emotions were battered. She'd walk willingly into Aiden's arms, but it would be without her heart. Damn his luck and damn his boss.

He listened as Roman explained what he already knew. Marshall was on his way. If he was lucky, he had thirty minutes to figure out how best to handle the situation.

"She's here," he announced into the phone before disconnecting the call.

She entered his office as he set the phone down.

"Hey, you made pretty good time."

She shrugged. Her eyes were tired and lacked the sparkle she normally had. "Do you have the list?"

He rose and walked around the desk. He pulled her into his arms, the move catching her off guard. "Sophie…"

Her shoulders sagged at his touch. "You heard everything, didn't you?"

"That's my job," he answered, leaning back to look down at her face. "Do I need to kill him?"

She shook her head. "No, but Aiden…You can cancel whatever training you have set up for me. I think this is my last case."

Aiden dropped his hold and stepped back. "You aren't a quitter. The Sophie I know wouldn't let any man run her off from doing what she was meant to do."

"Yeah, well I don't know what happened to that bitch."

"I do," he answered and pulled her in for another hug. "She was stupid and fell in love."

"Well, we can't all be perfect."

"I can." He winked and spread out the sheets in front of her with the list of names and corresponding faces of the people who'd entered the common area.

'You rock," she answered, leaning over the desk to get a closer look at the printed out pictures from the footage taken earlier in the day when Piper went missing.

Aiden stepped back around his desk and saw Marshall on the screen. He grabbed a pair of handcuffs out of his desk drawer and moved to stand next to Sophie. He leaned down next to her and whispered, "Don't hate me for this."

She glanced over at him. "What?"

She barely got the words out before he pressed his lips to hers while locking the cuff around her wrist. Before she even knew what was happening, Marshall grabbed him by the shirt and pulled him back. Aiden grinned and slapped the other cuff on his wrist before moving out of arm's reach. He'd cuffed the pair together, and from the looks on their faces, he was going to be dead when they got free.

They both glanced down at their chained wrists, each of them yanking in the opposite direction.

"Make up," Aiden announced. "Or you can spend the rest of the night cuffed together."

"You wouldn't." Sophie seethed through gritted teeth. She shoved their linked arms out for Aiden to unlock. "Take this off me now!"

Aiden shook his head and grinned. "No can do, sugar butt. Sometimes we all need a little help."

He grabbed the office keys out of his desk and stepped around the pair. He started to close the door. "I think you two are in desperate need of a time-out. I'll be back later to let you out."

"Paybacks are a bitch," she yelled at him as he pulled the door closed, locking them both inside.

****

Marshall's laughter filled the room.

"That son of a bitch. I'll kill him." Sophie felt the heat rising to her cheeks. She yanked her arm again. "Tell me you have a key."

Marshall grinned. "Nope."

"Why are you enjoying this? An hour ago you thought I was screwing him."

Marshall cupped her cheek with his free hand and she turned her face away.

"I'm sorry."

His words caught her off guard. Those were words she didn't hear often. Her brow rose but she remained quiet, not giving even an inch.

"I was scared, Sophie. I was scared that I wasn't good enough. I was scared that I was going to lose you. I was scared that you had almost died because of me. So I did the only thing I could think of."

"You pushed me away," she answered for him. Her voice came out a whisper.

"I pushed you away."

Every fiber of her being wanted to believe him. Believe the words he was telling her.

"You said you'd never lie to me."

"I didn't lie to you. I used Aiden's attraction to you to my advantage. I never said you were screwing him. I didn't know how else to drive you away."

"That's cheap, Marshall."

"I needed to make you mad. I needed to give you a reason to give up on me." Marshall rested his palm on her face again, only this time she leaned into his warmth. "I'm so sorry. I was a jerk and I'll spend the rest of my life making it up to you."

Sophie let out a deep breath and her gaze held his. "Don't do it again."

"I won't," he answered while yanking their joined hands, pulling her against his body. He pressed his lips to hers in a kiss that spoke volumes about his regret.

He rested his forehead against hers. "What were you doing here? We have a ceremony to attend tomorrow."

Sophie turned toward the desk. "These are pictures of everyone who entered and exited the third floor. I thought if we could figure out who trashed Piper's apartment, then we'd be closer to the killer."

Marshall picked up another piece of paper. It was the list of eighteen coven members with military experience. Eight of the names were highlighted. "Why are some of them highlighted?"

"I asked him to do backgrounds on who might have medical and explosive training. In the picture provided of Mary, there was a pinprick in her neck. I think she may have been drugged."

"You think it was one of these names?"

She raised the hand with the cuff before remembering that she should use the other one. She slipped the list out of his hands. She knew every highlighted name except two. They ranged from old to young. Winnie, Franklin and Kevin were just a few of the highlighted names on the list.

"Looks like you're marrying me," Marshall announced. "The mountain man made the list."

"It doesn't mean he's the killer."

"It doesn't mean he's not the killer. We need to get you back to the coven."

She wiggled the cuffs and pointed toward the door. "How are we going to do that?"

Marshall grinned as he pulled out the key ring from the SUV he'd arrived in. On it was a handcuff key. He slid it into the lock and turned, the cuff falling free from her wrist.

"You weren't going to tell me, were you?"

"Nope," he answered.

Marshall pulled out his weapon and shot at the doorknob; the door swung free on the hinges. "Did you honestly think a locked door would have stopped me for long?"

She smirked. "I guess nothing stops you if you're determined."

She rounded the desk and clicked on the keyboard.

"What are you doing?"

"Just leaving Aiden a little present on his computer." Three more clicks and she picked up the papers and pictures on the desk.

Aiden appeared in the doorway with a coffee cup in hand.

"Was that necessary?" he asked while gesturing toward the swinging door.

"Absolutely." Marshall grinned, placing his palm on Sophie's back. He led her out into the hallway, but she paused out of sight.

"What…"

She shushed him and wiggled her brows.

"Gay porn, gay porn," the computer speakers announced, the volume as loud as she could turn it. "This user is watching gay porn." Sounds of men moaning filled the room.

"What the hell," Aiden growled.

She chuckled and kept walking.

"You're vicious."

"Oh honey, I'm just getting started." She grinned and kept walking.

11 CHAPTER

Sophie stretched her arms above her head before rolling and tossing her arm across Marshall's body. She glanced up at him. His eyes were open and he grinned. "Good morning, wife."

"Good morning, husband." She snuggled into his embrace. "We're getting married today."

Piper's apparition appeared in the room. Her confused gaze met Sophie's. Sophie's heart sank into her stomach and dread filled her veins. Sophie pulled the sheet up to cover her chest. "Oh no, not you too."

Marshall glanced around the room. "Who's here?"

"Piper," Sophie said, sitting up and taking the sheet with her. "What happened to you?"

Piper's eyes were sad. She didn't say a word. Her hand went to her bare neck as she held Sophie's gaze. The leader's pendant was missing. She vanished just as fast as she appeared.

Sophie heart clenched tighter. "She's dead."

Marshall sat up next to her, his fingers rubbing a soothing circle on Sophie's back.

"She had a vision the first time. She left me a note. She must not have seen this one coming."

"We'll catch this guy." Marshall pulled Sophie into his embrace. "Nothing is going to happen to you. I won't let it."

Sophie raised her hand to her neck. "She was missing her pendant. Whoever is doing this must be keeping them as souvenirs and used Mary's to shift suspicion."

Marshall slid out of the bed and held out his hand to Sophie, as if trying to lighten the mood. "How about one last fling before you're a married woman?"

"We have to find Piper." Sophie's brows dipped, ignoring his hand.

"We will; I promise," he answered leaning over and pressing his lips to hers. "After we're married."

She pulled him down on top of her and kissed him back. "After we're married."

****

Sophie zipped up the coven's standard white dress hoping that was the outfit of choice for their weddings. The bodice was beautiful and embroidered with intricate design work. It didn't do much to show off her figure, but it was pretty, clean and innocent. She twisted her hair up in a pretty do, adjusting it in place. She swiped the last of her makeup across her lips and stared at her reflection.

Butterflies took flight in her stomach. She was getting married, and not only that, it was a sham. When had her life changed to make something like that acceptable?

"You were lost the first time he kissed you," Will answered from behind her.

She spun around to face her spirit guide. "You show up now...after everything!"

"I show up when you need me. Saved your husband, didn't I?" he quipped.

She pulled the bathroom door open and walked out into the room. "Fine. Are you ready to tell me who the killer is?"

She slipped on a pair of flats, which would be hidden beneath the floor-length dress.

"You need to wear boots."

"Boots beneath my dress? Have you lost your mind?"

"No, but you'll thank me later."

"Do I need my gun too?"

He nodded, his lips turned down in a frown.

"Shit." She plopped down on the bed. "Something is going to happen, isn't it?"

He nodded again. "I've said too much. I have to go."

"Wait..." she yelled before he vanished.

****

Marshall held Sophie's hand as they followed the other dressed-up men and women wearing white toward the common area. The big, happy ceremony was to happen at dusk after a quick coven meeting. She wasn't a member yet, but anyone and everyone taking part in the big shindig was required to attend and their guests were allowed to go to the meeting.

The round dining tables were replaced with row after row of chairs. Standing at the platform were her neighbor -Ted, Nana, and another woman whom Sophie hadn't seen before. Ted and Nana were in a heated discussion as the other woman just listened. Ted was speaking through gritted teeth, yet the way he poked at the book in his hand spoke volumes as he leaned toward the older woman's face. Nana was smiling back at him and shaking her head, disagreeing with whatever he had to say.

Marshall gestured to the chairs in the back row. Roman and Dash waited, leaning against the back wall. They garnished several looks from the residents. The women were smitten. A few stopped to talk to them and quickly turned to glance at Sophie.

Marshall leaned toward Sophie's ear, his arm going around her chair. "I'm guessing you just made some new best friends."

Sophie grinned. "Just wait until I tell them all that my cousins are gay."

Marshall chuckled as he glanced over his shoulder, his voice barely above a whisper. "They aren't gay."

Sophie leaned into her husband as if to kiss his cheek and whispered back, "You know that, and I know that, but the others don't. They are still giving me hell over all of the noise we make in the room. Since this is my sting, I say they're gay. So they're gay."

She pressed a quick kiss to her husband's cheek before turning to face the front of the room. She smiled as she folded her hands in her lap, silently pleased with her fake cousins' new sexual preferences. Turnabout was fair play, and it was time they all realized she wouldn't take any more of their jokes.

Sophie scanned the room and her smile slipped. Men and women filled the once empty chairs. Even though every chair was full, the place didn't feel as crowded as it normally did. The breathing room was throwing her off her game. Something was missing. Sophie chewed her lips as she took in everyone around her. No spirits were in attendance. None were checking on their charges. None even flashed into the room for a brief second. It was devoid of other-worldly visitors.

Sophie leaned into her husband again to whisper. "There aren't any of the see-through kind in attendance."

"Is that weird?" Marshall asked, using his fingers to draw circles on her sleeve.

"I don't know. Will warned me to wear my boots and carry my weapon. Be prepared for anything," she answered, her brows dipped between her eyes. Between the ominous warning and lack of transparent spirits in the room, every nerve ending in her body was now on alert. She straightened in her chair, uncrossing her legs. She wrung her fingers together as she scanned her surroundings once more.

The unknown older woman standing on the platform moved in front of the podium. If Piper had an air of authority about her, then this woman looked as though she controlled the world. She seethed of confidence and her hazel eyes twinkled with wisdom. She cleared her throat and smiled.

"Good evening."

"Good evening," was chorused back.

"My name is Helena-Marie Blansett. I'm the presiding mayor and coven leader in Blansett, North Carolina. Due to coven requirements and guidelines, I'm stepping in as headmistress to oversee your voting process due to Piper Gray's disappearance. It's been brought to my attention that there are three families eligible, due to their lineage."

Sophie's throat went dry. Her fingers stilled.

"The nominees are Winnie Hathaway, Vivian Baxter and Sophie Dixon. Their ancestors can be traced back through our covens for over fifty years, making all of them eligible to assume the role."

Sophie's mouth fell open and she met Ted's gaze. He waved a book in the air and his brow wiggled up and down.

Sophie shook her head, fast and furious. Her eyes widened in horror.

Marshall leaned into her. "I guess you should have stopped by to see what the hell our neighbor had on your history."

"I guess so," she murmured back.

"Voting will commence after the renewal of vows and the reception." Helena-Marie quieted the whispers spreading throughout the room. Several residents turned to meet Sophie's gaze, looks of utter confusion on their faces, which matched the turmoil running rampant in Sophie's mind.

"All of the married members will meet in the sacred ritual field behind the pavilion where the blessings will take place. All non-married members will meet back in the common area an hour later. Are there any questions?"

Nana's nephew, Franklin, rose from his chair. "Sophie Dixon is not fit to run as our leader. She doesn't know our ways, even if her ancestors did."

"Get ready to pay up," Marshall whispered. "The woodsman just nailed the coffin shut."

Sophie rolled her eyes.

"She can learn. Her lineage requires that she be included in the vote. If you or any of the others don't think she can do the job, then it's your right as members to vote for someone you believe can fill the role. Her name is still up for consideration." Helena-Marie Blansett gave Franklin a hard stare. The look would make most men slink back into line and Franklin was no exception. Sophie marveled at the woman's strength.

Sophie's stomach rolled. She wasn't a leader, least of all *their* leader.

"Since there are no more questions, we'll convene for the festivities."

Helena-Marie stepped down off the podium and proceeded down the aisle. She stopped in front of the row where Marshall and Sophie sat. "Mrs. Dixon, may I have a word?"

"Sure," Sophie answered as she stood. She shrugged at Marshall as she excused herself and followed the woman out of the building. Marshall walked to the back of the room with Dash and Roman and followed slowly behind her and Helena-Marie.

Helena-Marie walked in step with Sophie toward the field behind the pavilion. "I knew your grandmother."

"Well, at least that makes one of us," Sophie answered with a fake smile.

"She was a strong woman, an even stronger medium." Helena gave a sideways glance at Sophie. "It was my understanding that neither your grandmother nor your mom wanted this for you."

Sophie stopped walking and Helena stopped too.

"What, are you surprised?"

"You said my mother. My mother didn't have abilities."

"Of course she did. Every female in your line has them."

"Wait...how do you know that?"

Helena-Marie wrapped her arm around Sophie's and started leading her toward the sacred clearing. "I know all, dear; it's part of my ability. To understand what hasn't been said. To read a person's character before they utter the first syllable. It's a blessing and a curse."

"How is that possible?"

"The same way it's possible for you to travel between realities." She glanced at Sophie. "That's what it is when you're yanked away. You're in the layer between here and the other side. It's a meeting place. The spirits and your guides will show you places and things when you need to see them, or just let you see the void when they want to talk."

"The white room," Sophie mumbled, her mind immediately going back to that time and space when the last spirit had whisked her away for a chat. Marshall and Jack's best friend had tried to warn her of things that were coming. "If what you said is true, then you know why I'm here."

"I do."

"Then why didn't you say something?"

"I learned early on that I shouldn't mess with divine purpose. Warning others would be like cheating them out of the lessons they need to learn. It would be giving them Cliff Notes to avoid the highs and lows of life. They wouldn't learn a thing while they were here, and in turn, the same experience would be much harder in their next life." She shrugged. "Besides, I don't want to screw with my own karma."

"I can see why you're a mayor."

"It's more than seeing what can't be seen, dear. It's having faith and determination in the people around you. For others, that is a blind faith, for me not so much." She grinned. "I think it's time your fake license becomes real. Let's go get you married."

Sophie's mouth parted. This woman did know more than she could see. Sophie was trying to digest the information as they stepped around the pavilion into the clearing. Little white lights were strung into the nearby trees, making the place look magical. White chiffon was strung at the end of the rows of chairs outside of the circle. The same material was strung from the pillars that made an enclosed circle. Flowers and salt were spread on the ground surrounding the pillars, and Sophie knew immediately it was a sacred spot. She could feel the powerful energy in the air. Spirits from generations past were standing behind the circle. Why they hadn't been in the meeting room was a mystery. It was possible they didn't want to interfere with the choices being suggested, regardless, she'd probably never know. Many ghostly faces Sophie didn't recognize, but yet she knew who they were. Will was among them. He held Sophie's stare, and sadness filled his eyes. He wasn't happy like the rest.

Helena-Marie led Sophie through the already assembling crowd and up to the front of the platform. "You and Marshall should stand here." She smiled before taking her place on the platform. Marshall reached her and pulled her into his embrace. He kissed her, his eyes searching hers. "You don't have to do this."

"Are you backing out on me, Mr. Dixon?"

"Mrs. Dixon, I plan to love you for a million lifetimes."

Sophie rested one hand on her stomach and the other was clutched around Marshall's palm. Helena-Marie called the ceremony to order. She read from a book and gave a nice sermon on the meaning of marriage before she completed the group vows. Sophie repeated the words while gazing into Marshall's eyes. Her sight was clouded in tears as she looked up at him. His love shone back at her as he repeated the vows, promising to love her and cherish her till death do them part.

Helena-Marie announced, "You can now kiss your spouse," and what Sophie thought to be cheers at first were actually gunfire coming from the direction of the trees. She watched as Helena-Marie dove to the right, her eyes trained on Sophie's face. Screams rent the air as men and women dove around them. Another shot and the man beside Marshall fell to his knees, cupping his shoulder. Blood soaked his white dress shirt.

Marshall yanked Sophie to the ground, covering her body as he pulled his weapon, squeezing off a shot toward the woods.

Chaos ensued around them as husbands and wives ran from the site. Sophie sat up and looked around the area. Vivian was lying on the ground with a bullet wound to her leg as others surrounded her, trying to help pull her away. On the podium, Helena-Marie had collapsed. Sophie rushed to her side as Roman and Dash came running up with their weapons drawn. Helena-Marie was clutching her shoulder and she smiled though her grimace.

Helena had blocked a shot that would have hit Sophie.

Sophie pressed her hand to Helena's shoulder, stopping the flow of blood. "You knew. That's why you wanted me in front of the podium."

Helena gave a devious smile but didn't deny or accept that her actions had been deliberate.

"It ends today," Helena announced. "I'll be fine. You have to go."

Sophie grabbed Dash by the arm and yanked him down next to her. "Get her help."

He nodded and lifted the woman off the ground, carrying her away in his arms.

12 CHAPTER

Sophie pulled the concealed Glock from her leg holster. Marshall sent Roman in one direction and Sophie in the other direction. He went up the middle. The idea was to flush the shooter out. There was no way this person was going to slip past them. Helena-Marie was right. This ended today. Sophie clutched her dress, lifting it above her feet while holding the gun in her hand. She took off at a run in the direction Marshall had pointed. She reached the tree line without a shot being fired.

She stepped into the green foliage, stepping over fallen limbs as she held the gun up to her chest, her gaze assessing. A bird flapped from a nearby branch, flying off into the air. The hair on Sophie's neck was standing on end. She eased her way through the forest, letting her gaze travel over the vines and weeds. The trees were covered in green leaves with hints of red and orange marking the change in seasons. Sophie moved rhythmically through the forest. Branches cracked in the distance, making her pause. Her heart threatened to burst from her chest. The pounding of the blood in her veins made her head ache, but her fingers remained tight around the grip of her gun.

They didn't have earpieces to hear each other. The forest was lonely yet alive with animals. The lowering sun was covered by the green trees overhead. This wasn't an ideal situation for any of them, let alone a woman in a long white dress.

Piper appeared, her see-through outline superimposed over the trunk of a tree. She pointed in the direction that Marshall had taken and raised her hand to her neck.

"Who is it?" Sophie asked, without moving.

Piper pointed over and over again in the same direction, never uttering a sound.

Sophie started off in Marshall's direction, ignoring her husband's original command. "I hope you're right," she mumbled as she moved across the forest horizontally to get to the path Marshall had taken.

She slowed at the sound of voices. Marshall's voice. "Why are you doing this?"

Sophie inched closer to the voices before crouching down behind a large tree trunk. She peered around the corner. A woman, with a log at her feet, stood holding a gun. Marshall was on the ground, his gun two feet from his body.

"You should have never come here," Winnie yelled before she pulled the trigger. The shot rang out in the early night air.

"No!" Sophie screamed and stepped out from behind the tree, her gaze holding Winnie's as she moved closer to Marshall.

He was lying on his back. Blood seeped from his side, making his shirt red. His eyes were closed, his body motionless.

"Drop it, Winnie." Sophie narrowed her eyes. The tension in the air thickened. There was no way this bitch was getting away with shooting her husband.

"Fitting you should die with your husband." Winnie smirked.

"Why are you doing this?"

"You didn't deserve the role of leader. You don't even have a fucking clue what you're doing, none of the assholes we killed did. We did the other covens a favor by getting rid of their trash. Now it's time for ours."

"I just found out about my lineage." Sophie tilted her head. "But you knew, didn't you? That's why you've been gunning for me since I got here."

Winnie smirked. "Vivian knew and had her sons digging through the archives to find the information on your mother. She knew the moment she saw you."

"You're killing because you want to be a leader and what....rule the world?"

"We've aligned leaders in all of the covens throughout the eastern portion of the United States; soon enough, we'll control them all."

Sophie chuckled. "And what? Cast some spells? Do you think that running the coven really gives you that much power?"

"Our reach goes beyond the covens. Think of all of the people in the covens and their jobs outside of the properties. We have politicians, lawyers, even the police in our pocket."

"So it's like a secret society." Sophie pressed her lips together. "Well, I guess once we stop you, we've got more work to do."

"You won't stop me."

Breaking branches behind Winnie caused Sophie's heart to race. Kevin circled Winnie's waist and kissed her neck. "That's right, baby. It's all ours, and with the others in place, we'll rule the world."

"Ours?" Winnie asked, disdain on her face. "I don't think so."

She turned and fired her weapon at Kevin's chest before she jerked back around to face Sophie. "The stupid schmuck thought I was going to marry him and have babies."

Winnie shivered. "As if that was going to happen. I might as well take out all of Vivian's line in one night. Don't you agree?"

"You won't get away with this."

Sophie heard the rustle of leaves behind her. She moved to the right, keeping an eye on the newcomer, along with Winnie. Franklin joined the party. Winnie's gun shifted back and forth between Sophie and Franklin.

"Not you too?" Sophie whined.

Franklin's jaw set to stone when he noticed his brother on the ground. He shifted the axe he was carrying in his hand.

"No, not me too," spewed from gritted teeth. He lifted his axe.

Franklin threw the blade through the air at the same time Sophie fired.

Winnie shot in Franklin's direction as Sophie dove to the ground for cover.

The bullet hit Winnie's head as the axe embedded in her heart. The momentum of the axe and the bullet thrust Winnie's body backwards before it landed with a thud on the forest floor.

"Are you all right?" Franklin asked as he fell to his knees, cupping his shoulder.

Sophie nodded, unable to speak. She scurried to Marshall's side and ripped his shirt open. His entire side was covered in blood, the bullet hole evident. She ripped the bottom portion of her dress and used it as a compress to staunch the blood flow.

"Marshall," she called out. He didn't move. She felt for a pulse, relieved even though it was faint. The small movement in his chest gave her a little hope but fear at the same time.

His eyes slid open and he held her gaze before briefly shutting them again. Her heart started beating in that moment, though the tears still streamed down her face.

"Oh no you don't." She grabbed his jaw. "You aren't going anywhere. You're not allowed. I won the bet and the only thing I want is for you to live." She pressed her lips to his. His eyes remained closed. "Do you hear me? I need you to live. I love you."

Roman came running out through a clump of trees, sliding to a halt. His phone pressed against his ear. She ignored his shouts of life flight and ambulances, refusing to believe that Marshall was going to die.

Minutes, that seemed like hours, ticked by before she heard the whip of a helicopter's blades. Roman had moved her out of the way to access the damage. Her hands and dress were stained with Marshall's blood. She sat back on her knees, knowing that her legs wouldn't hold her as she gazed around at the carnage. Marshall was carried out of the woods on a body board while some of the coven members and people from the chopper checked Winnie and Franklin.

She couldn't move. She didn't dare move. If she moved, then it meant that everything was real.

Roman squeezed her shoulders and raised her off the ground. "You're in shock."

She didn't speak. She couldn't.

"It's okay. I've got you," Roman announced as he scooped her up into his arms. Sophie closed her eyes, wishing she would wake up and discover it had just been a dream. A nightmare that she'd just witnessed.

"Roman, you and Mrs. Dixon need to come with us," a guy from the helicopter crew announced as Roman carried her through the field where she'd just said her vows. Till death do us part. She'd promised till death do us part.

Will appeared next to her in the helicopter transport. "Snap out of it, Sophie. He hasn't transitioned to our side yet. He's fighting it."

Those words got her attention, pulling her from the dark place her thoughts were taking her. She turned her head to look at him. "Thank you."

The medics ignored her as they worked on saving Marshall's life. Roman held Sophie pulled into his side, his hold tight, secure and safe. She let the tears fall and her body shook. She'd almost lost Marshall before she ever really had him.

****

Sophie waited in the surgical ICU with the rest of the team. They'd brought her a change of clothes and Amber. Amber and Sophie clutched each other and they cried together. There were no questions, just the silent support from her best friend. Jack was in the waiting room, sitting next to Dash. He'd met her gaze on a couple of occasions and all Sophie could do was look away. She couldn't face him, not now.

The physician walked into the room and pulled the surgical mask down from around his mouth. "Mrs. Dixon?" he asked as he looked around.

Sophie stood, unsure if her legs would hold her. "Yes."

The doctor moved to stand in front of her. "We've done what we can. We've stopped the bleeding and repaired what we could. We won't know his prognosis until he wakes up. I'm sorry."

Sophie's legs gave out and Jack caught her, helping her stand.

"Can I see him?" she asked.

The doctor glanced around the room as all of the men stood. Their presence alone would have frightened lesser men.

"You are going to let her see him," Roman announced and stepped forward.

"I'm sure he is," Aiden agreed and stepped to stand behind Sophie.

"He'd be a fool not to," Beau threw in for good measure.

"If he's smart he will." Amber stepped up next to Sophie, her arms crossed over her chest.

"Of course," the doctor announced and led Sophie out of the room. He used his badge to open the double mechanical doors and ushered her into the ICU. Even though the rooms were separated, they didn't have doors. The nurses could look into each room from the nurses' area stationed in the middle.

He gestured her into one of the rooms and Sophie had to steel her legs. Marshall was lying on the bed with tubes and lines running into his body and out every which way. His normally tan face was pale and his eyes were closed. Monitors next to the bed beeped, and the lines on the screen went up and down in a rhythm that told her it was his heartbeat.

Sophie inhaled a deep breath and moved to the side of the bed. She took his hand in hers and pressed a kiss to his forehead.

"Only a few minutes."

She nodded, although they were going to have to physically remove her from the room before she ever went willingly.

Sophie leaned over and pressed her lips to the side of his. "Marshall, baby, can you hear me?"

She received no answer. No tightening of the hold on her hand, no blinking of eyes, nothing to indicate that he could hear anything going on around him.

She leaned her forehead against his and cupped his cheek. The warmth from his skin reminded her that he was fighting.

"I love you." She closed her eyes. "Marshall, please come back." She pressed another kiss to his face. "Please wake up," she begged. "I can't do this without you."

His fingers twitched in hers, but his eyes stayed closed. She stilled, concentrating on their connection.

"You can hear me?" she whispered in his ear. "I love you."

His fingers twitched again and his eyes slid open. "I lost the bet."

Sophie's whole body shook as she fought the tears. Relief coursed through her body. "Yes, you lost."

He cleared his throat and coughed. "I never go back on a bet."

Sophie called for the doctor and the nurses. Several entered the room and it took some very big orderlies to escort her out of the ICU and back to the waiting room.

She visited him every day as they moved him from ICU into a regular room. The guys were there as much as she was. They never had a minute to themselves.

Marshall insisted they get back to business as usual. She'd driven out to the coven to assess the aftermath and to figure out where Piper's body was. She was pleased to find that Nana was okay and she'd stepped up as leader until another younger person could be sought. She wore black to grieve the death of her nephew and she'd kept Franklin close during the visit.

Where there had once been betrayal now stood a camaraderie that would strengthen the foundation. Winnie and Kevin hadn't broken the spirit of the coven. They'd made them stronger. The authorities found the medallions in Kevin's room among the shrine he'd made with Winnie as the star. Helen-Marie Blansett had made Sophie promise to come visit her quaint little town when things settled. Her wound was minor and easily healed compared to the others.

Sophie returned to the office before calling it a night and heading home, their weekly meetings rescheduled as Marshall recuperated at home.

"Sophie, can you meet me in the conference room?" Aiden asked as he walked by her office.

"Sure," she answered and followed behind. She turned the corner and found Aiden and another man who looked just like him staring back at her. The only difference was the color of their eyes. Aiden had green and his brother had blue.

"You must be the triplet I haven't met."

"Alexander. It's nice to meet you." He held out his hand and she shook it. "You must be the infamous Sophie. I've heard a lot about you."

"All good I hope."

Alexander made a sour face.

"Everything he heard was from Alexis," Aiden said, responding to the funny look.

Sophie grinned. "She still talks about me? I must have ruffled her feathers."

"You could say that," Alexander answered and gestured to the papers on the table. "Mr. Dixon asked that I bring these to you to expedite the process."

Sophie sat down in one of the chairs. Dissolution of Marriage scrolled across the top of the page. Her heart sank into her stomach. She glanced up at the men. "Marshall wanted this?"

Alexander nodded. "Yes. He's already signed them. He'd like this resolved by morning."

She flipped to the last page and bit her lip to fight back the tears that threatened to fall. Marshall had already signed. The marriage was a sham. She knew it and he knew it, but the reality of the papers rammed home the truth. She picked up the pen and scrolled her name, not caring what she'd just agreed to. She dropped the pen on top before sliding the tracking ring off her finger. She tossed that down too, before heading toward the door. She paused at the threshold and turned back toward Aiden. "Tell him it's done and I'm officially taking a vacation."

Alexander nodded as she left. She needed time so her heart could adjust. She hadn't even gotten used to the possibility of being married before it was yanked out from beneath her like a rug.

13 CHAPTER

"Dixon," Marshall said into his cell phone.

"Thanks, boss." Aiden chuckled.

"For what?" Marshall asked as he eased onto the bed.

"For putting her back on the market. As of tomorrow, you and she are no longer married."

"Aiden…" Marshall warned.

"Got to go. I'm sure she might need a shoulder to cry on."

Aiden hung up and Marshall got back off the bed. As much as he tried to hurry through the process of getting dressed, he wasn't moving as fast as he normally could. "Son of a bitch."

He took several deep breaths, breathing through the pain and called the only person who could help him.

Amber picked up on the first ring. "Sophie just signed the papers and I need you to run interference on Aiden until I can get everything lined up."

"You owe me," she answered in a sing-song voice.

"Agreed," he answered and set the phone back down, now taking his time to finish getting dressed. He called his driver to pick him up. He needed to act fast before he lost his opportunity.

****

Marshall clutched his side as he stood on Max Masterson's steps and rang the doorbell. Seconds ticked by until the door opened.

"Marshall, what are you doing here?"

"I need to talk to you."

Max stood back and waited for Marshall to enter. He led him to the study and waited as Marshall eased down into a seat. He breathed through the pain of the strain against his stitches.

"You shouldn't be out of bed."

"This is important."

Max poured himself a drink and handed Marshall a bottle of water before moving to sit behind his desk.

"Okay, shoot."

"Sophie and I filed for divorce." Marshall said.

He gave a slow nod. "Good."

"Not good. I love her and I believe she loves me. I came to—"

"Don't even say it."

"Max, I told you I'd do this right. I love her with every fiber of my being. She's it for me. There will never be another. I'm a man of my word and I'm asking for your blessing to make her my wife."

Max drained the glass in one swallow before he spoke again. "Does she want this?"

Marshall took a sip of the water. "I don't know. I haven't asked her yet. I hope she does."

Max leaned back in his chair, uncertainty written on his face. "You said you love her?"

"I do love her, and I need her like my next breath. I swear to take care of her, love her and protect her for the rest of my life."

Max's head drooped forward on his shoulders. "Marshall, she's my sister. She's the only one I have." He lifted his gaze to meet Marshall's. "If you ever hurt her, not even the law will stop me from returning the gesture. Are we clear?"

Marshall's lips tilted at the corner as he tried to fight the smile. "Crystal."

"Then I guess you have my blessing *if* she says yes." Max rose from seat and held out his hand. "Welcome to the family."

Marshall eased back out of his chair, careful of the stitches. "Can you and your wife come by the office tomorrow at ten?"

Max smiled, showing all of his teeth. "You're a brave man if you plan on doing this in front of an audience."

"I'd say I'm a braver man for where I have to go next."

Max led the way to the front door and pulled it open. "Jack?"

"Jack," Marshall echoed as he stepped out onto the stoop. "If I'm not in the office tomorrow, check the hospitals and the morgue."

"Good luck," Max called after him as Marshall eased down the steps.

"Thanks, I'm going to need it."

"You might want to go in armed," Max yelled back.

Marshall stood next to the driver, who had the back door opened. "I planned on it."

****

Marshall wasn't half as nervous about telling Sophie's brother as he was about telling his best friend. The pit of his stomach rolled and bile rose to his throat in anticipation of the first punch. Jack was standing at the front door when Marshall made it up the last step. His breath was already labored from the extra exertion he'd placed on himself.

"You look like shit," Jack announced.

"Feel like it too," Marshall answered back as he followed Jack into the house.

"Can I get you a beer?"

"Not tonight," Marshall answered as he followed his best friend into the kitchen.

Jack opened a beer before leaning against the kitchen counter. "What brings you by?"

"Sophie," Marshall answered without hesitation.

"What about her?"

"I signed the divorce papers today."

Jack took another swig of his beer. "And?"

"And I'm proposing to her tomorrow."

"You've got to be fucking kidding me." Jack threw his bottle against the wall. Shards of glass and beer covered the drywall. "Why her? She was mine."

"She loves me."

"She loved me first."

"I stayed away. You didn't trust her, and you royally screwed up when she saw the video of you kissing your ex."

Jack stormed forward stopping only when he was standing toe to toe with Marshall. "You know why I did that."

"I do." Marshall stood toe to toe with his best friend. "I didn't plan this."

"Of course you did," Jack shot back before walking over to the cabinet to pull down a bottle of Crown and a glass. He poured himself a double shot and downed it before filling the glass up again.

He rested his hands on the counter with his back to Marshall. "Don't ask me to be okay with this."

Marshall remained quiet. That was exactly what he'd been going to ask. "I don't know how to fix this between us. You're my brother from another mother, but she's my heart and my soul. She was the reason I kept fighting for my life in the hospital. A life I want to share with her."

Jack turned around to face Marshall. He crossed his arms over his chest. "Just go." Jack nodded toward the door. "Just go before I pound your ass. It's not a fair fight since you're crippled."

Marshall took two steps and turned around. "So what does this mean? You'll accept it?"

Jack shook his head. "No. Just means I won't hurt you today. I can't accept this. I won't accept this."

"You're going to have to."

"Not if she says no."

"I'm asking her tomorrow in our meeting at ten. Her family and friends will be there. I was hoping you would be too. You're the closest thing I have to family."

"Don't hold your breath." Jack walked out of the kitchen and disappeared into his room, slamming the door.

Marshall let himself out and climbed into the back seat before pulling out his phone. He dialed Amber's number again.

"Hello," she answered. The noise in the background was loud.

"I need another favor," Marshall announced.

"Just a minute. I need to walk outside."

Marshall listened to the rustle over the phone before the noise disappeared.

"Where are you?" he asked.

"The bar. She was depressed, so I got her out of the house. I figured I'd get her drunk and take her to my house so Aiden couldn't get his sexy-as-sin paws on her."

"Sexy paws?"

Amber chuckled. "What's your favor?'

"I need her in the office by ten. Can you make sure she comes in?"

"She claims to be on vacation. You might want to try sending one of the guys to pick her up from my house. You might have better luck if you claim to have an emergency. I know her bleeding heart can't pass up a person in trouble."

"Point taken. At least sober her up."

"I'll do my best," she answered before saying goodbye.

****

Sophie rolled over on the bed, snuggling into the plush comforter in Amber's spare bedroom. Sophie's head was throbbing in pain. She pulled the covers over her head, trying to block out the morning light from the sheer curtains.

"Rise and shine." Amber's cheerful voice was extra loud today.

"Go away," Sophie mumbled from beneath the sheets.

"You need to get in the shower."

Sophie felt something being set down on the bed. Sophie pulled the covers back to find Amber standing at the end of the bed, an extra pair of Sophie's clothes folded nicely nearby. "Beau called. There's an emergency at the office. They need you to go in."

She pulled the covers back over her head. "I'm on vacation."

Amber yanked the covers away. "He mentioned something about a majority vote. I'm not sure you can miss this, and I know you don't want smeared mascara on your face when Beau gets here to pick you up, so you might want to hurry."

Sophie frowned at her best friend.

"I'll make you some coffee while you transform into a knockout," she said in a chipper voice. "You're single now and I'm sure you want to look your best."

Sophie moaned while sliding out of the bed. She picked up the clothes at the end of her bed and padded into the bathroom to rinse away the beers she'd drunk last night. She was single again. Her heart felt heavy and her body limp as she moved through the functions of getting ready. Why hadn't he called her? Was he trying to push her away again? Stupid man. This was what she had feared from the beginning, but if he thought to run her out of the company by vote, he was mistaken. She was a partner and she'd warned him before starting the relationship.

She took her shower and put on some makeup before tossing her hair up in a ponytail. The need to feel pretty wasn't at the top on her priority list. Getting through the day around the guys and Marshall was the only thing she wanted to accomplish. She got dressed and drank her coffee while waiting for Beau to show up. Absentmindedly she ran her thumb across the bottom of her ring finger. The smooth skin felt bare, her hand lighter without the weight of the ring.

Beau picked her up and the atmosphere was strained between him and Amber. Sophie climbed into the big monster truck.

"What gives?" she asked as she buckled her seatbelt.

He glanced at her. "I don't know why we're meeting. Marshall mentioned a man on the verge of losing his life."

"I meant with you and Amber. I must be the worst best friend in the world not to have even noticed."

"Nah." He tossed the truck into gear, the loud engine rumbling, before he threw it into gear taking them further down the road and away from the comfortable bed where she'd planned to sleep off her hangover.

"Neither of us was in it for a relationship. We just went our separate ways. No big deal."

Sophie's mouth dropped open. "Does she know that?"

He chuckled. "It was her idea. Something about taking a sabbatical from all men. We were never serious."

Sophie's lips dipped into a frown. She'd been so self-absorbed in her own life she hadn't seen what was going on with her friend.

"You aren't interested anymore?"

He shook his head. "Nope. No desire for the white picket fence."

"Huh. I used to have that same attitude until I experienced a glimpse of what it would be like with Marshall."

"And now?"

She shrugged. "I can see myself married one day, even if it's not with him." Her voice got softer as she finished the sentence. The rest of the ride was in silence until he parked in the garage and killed the engine.

"Hopefully, it will be a short meeting and you can get back to your vacation."

"That would be nice," she mumbled as she pushed the button to call the elevator. "Do you know anything else about this case?"

"Nope. Just that this client is a rich and lucky son of a bitch."

They stepped into the elevator and hit the button for the floor they needed. "Doesn't sound too lucky if he needs our help."

Beau's lips tilted in a smirk. "Sounds like he brought all of this on himself. Lost something he once had. If you ask me, he deserves a little bit of misery."

The elevator dinged, announcing their arrival before it slid open.

"Marshall seems to think that you'll be the only one who can help him."

Sophie brows dipped as they headed down the hall toward the conference room.

She walked into the room and found her partners and her family sitting around the table. Her gaze met Marshall's and her world stood still. He was dressed in slacks and a button-down shirt. He stood tall and proud, even though she could feel the pain from his wound as if it were her own. "Sophie."

She ignored him and turned toward her brother. "What are you doing here?"

Max nodded toward Marshall. "I think he should be the one to tell you."

She stepped farther into the room and sat in the seat that Beau pulled out for her. Beau sat her in the chair right next to Marshall.

Marshall cleared his throat. "This is a special meeting." He nodded toward Max and Eileen. "Thank you both for coming."

Max nodded with a scowl on his face as Eileen smiled on.

"We have a situation and a client needs our help, and I'm afraid that Sophie is the only one who can help this man."

Sophie brows rose. "Oh?"

"I'm afraid the poor bastard lost something very special to him."

"I heard he gave it away," Aiden chimed in.

"Ha, I heard he never had it to begin with." Roman chuckled.

"I heard he was a schmuck for letting it go," Dash chimed in.

"Yeah, well I heard he stole it from the beginning," Jack said from behind her. Amber was standing next to him. Amber's mouth fell open before she smacked him in the ribs.

Sophie glanced around the room at her partners. "What's going on? Who is the client and what did he lose?"

Marshall rounded the table and got down on one knee. She knew the move hurt him from the wince he was trying to hide on his face. A face she knew as well as her own.

"What are you doing?" she asked. "You shouldn't be down there. You're going to pull your stitches."

He took her hand and held her gaze. "I'm the client and you're the owner of my heart. Sophie, I know the way we started out wasn't conventional, but one look at you and I knew you were the one for me." He grinned. "It may have taken you a little longer, but not me. I love you with all of my heart, Sophie Masterson, and I'll spend the rest of my life trying to be the man you need me to be. You're the air I need to breathe and the sun that fills my days. I can't imagine living another day without you as a partner by my side, not just in business, but in life." He pulled a box out of his pocket and opened it up. It was his grandmother's ring. The beautiful one she'd refused to wear. The family heirloom that had been passed down through generations.

Sophie felt the tears welling up in her eyes. Butterflies erupted in her belly.

"Marry me, for real this time, and be my wife?" he asked.

A tear trickled down her cheek. He was proposing in front of God and everyone. Everyone who mattered most to her in the world. A pin drop could be heard around the room as they collectively held their breaths. He was asking for forever and in their line of work that could be tomorrow. There was nothing certain. The only thing she'd learned was that life was too short not to live each day to the fullest. She loved him, and unable to deny the truth, she answered.

"Yes. Yes." She leaned forward and smashed her lips against his in a kiss that she hoped conveyed her answer. "I love you," she said again against his lips before she leaned back.

He took the ring out of the box and slid it onto her finger. The feel was similar, yet different from the tracker she'd worn before. She wore this one out of love, instead of necessity.

Cheers filled the room as Marshall stood and pulled Sophie up into his arms. The guys joked and teased. She glanced toward the door. Jack held her gaze. She could read the grief in his eyes, the acceptance that their relationship was over. He gave a small nod before turning and walking away.

She turned her gaze to Amber and grinned. "You knew?"

She nodded; her smile was big and bright.

Sophie turned to her brother. "And you?"

He nodded. "He asked me first."

Her heart broke open a little more with the admission. Marshall truly loved her to ask permission and then to turn around and tell Jack. She turned in his arms and kissed his lips once more. "Why the divorce?"

"Our previous marriage was based on a sham. I wanted you to have the real thing this time."

She kissed him again. Champagne appeared along with flutes and a two-tiered cake with plates and forks.

"You did all this?" she asked, leaning into his embrace. "What if I had said no?"

"I would have worn you down." He winked. "I love you."

14 CHAPTER

The wedding was big and beautiful and everything Sophie hadn't realized she wanted. Sophie stood at the bar during the reception and watched everyone she loved enjoying themselves. The party was winding down now. Amber was on the dance floor with Aiden. His hands roamed down over her ass as she constantly fought to bring them back up to her waist. Her face was red, her eyes narrowed. She wasn't enjoying herself. She shoved against his chest and tried to retreat, but he twirled her back against his chest. "Well, that's interesting."

"Are you happy?" Jack asked as he walked over to her. He was dressed in a tuxedo, having agreed to be Marshall's best man. When Sophie had found them months later in the sparring room, he'd been sporting a cut lip and bleeding nose, and Marshall had an ugly black eye. They were both exhausted and heaving for breath when she had broken them up, all of the fight gone. He'd agreed but under duress. Sophie hoped one day his resentment would go away.

Sophie watched as Marshall cut in to dance with Amber, saving her, like the man she'd hoped he would be. "Yes," she answered before turning to meet his gaze. "Are you okay?"

He shrugged and took a swig of his beer. "I've been better." Jack gestured toward the dance floor. "He's a good man."

"I know," she answered, turning back to find Marshall batting at Aiden's hands as he tried to steal back his dance partner.

"If it wasn't me, I'm glad it's him." Jack tossed his arm around Sophie's shoulders and kissed her forehead. "I think my date is getting jealous."

Jack gestured toward the table where Alexis sat with her other brother, Alexander.

"I can't believe you brought her." Sophie smacked him in the gut. "She hates me."

He grinned. "She doesn't hate you. She hates not getting her way. She's really a nice girl and you might like her if you ever got to know her."

Sophie couldn't hide her smirk. "That's a bit of a stretch."

"Maybe," he answered as he walked off, leaving Sophie by herself. She turned her gaze back to her husband. All of the guys were taking turns dancing with Amber, keeping Aiden away. Beau stood across the room with two blonde bombshells on his arm.

"It looks like you found your way," Will announced, appearing beside her.

Sophie smiled. "Might have been easier had you given me a map."

"And miss the fireworks?" he asked. "The fun is just beginning."

Sophie turned to find a devious smile plastered on his lips.

"What?" she asked.

He placed his transparent hand on her belly. "There's someone waiting anxiously to meet you." He winked. "Enjoy your sleep for the next nine months. You won't be getting much more your entire life."

Will vanished out of sight, leaving Sophie at a loss for words.

"Shit."

"Language, Mrs. Dixon." Marshall pulled her into his arms. "Whose ass do I need to kick?"

She grinned. "Will just left, with some interesting parting words."

"Oh?" he asked, leaning down to kiss her neck. "Did he come to wish us well or tell us there is more chaos in our future?"

"You might say that." She leaned away from his lips, meeting his gaze. "Depends on whether you think babies and diapers are chaos."

His grin grew wide and his eyes twinkled. "That's the best kind of chaos."

He leaned down and kissed her like his life depended on it. Love exploded in her heart. Her world and life were finally in line. Marshall loved her; her family and friends supported her; and she finally believed in herself. Yes, everything was right in her world.

The End

ABOUT THE AUTHOR

Kate has lived in Florida for most of her entire life. She enjoys a quiet life with her husband, Michael and two kids.

Kate has pulled all-nighters finishing her favorite books and also writing them. She says she'll sleep when she's dead or when her muse stops singing off key.

She loves creating worlds full of suspense, secrets, hunky men, kick ass heroines, steamy sex and oh yeah the love of a lifetime. Not to mention an occasional ghost and other supernatural talents thrown into the mix.